His heart stood still and his breath lodged in his lungs. Everything around him seemed to freeze. *No. It couldn't be.* **"How old is Lolly?"**

"Does it matter?" Charlie spun and walked toward the door. "If you want to see the threats, follow me."

He caught her arm and pulled her around to face him, his fingers digging into her skin. "How old is she?" he demanded, his lips tight, a thousand thoughts spinning in his head, zeroing in on one.

For a long moment, she met his gaze, refusing to back down. Finally, she tilted her chin upward a fraction and answered, "Six."

"Just six?" His gut clenched.

"Six and a few months."

Her words hit him like a punch in the gut. Ghost fought to remain upright when he wanted to double over with the impact. Instead, he dropped his hands to his sides and balled his fists. "Is she—"

"Yours?" She shrugged. "Does it matter? Will it change anything?"

HOT COMBAT

New York Times Bestselling Author

ELLE JAMES

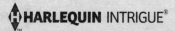

HARLEQUIN INTRIGUE®

This book is dedicated to my three lovely writing friends who encouraged me to write like my fingers were on fire during our annual writing retreat. If not for them and the timing of the retreat, this book might not have been written! Thank you, Cynthia D'Alba, Parker Kincade and Mandy Harbin.

ISBN-13: 978-1-335-72078-8

Recycling programs
for this product may
not exist in your area.

Hot Combat

Copyright © 2017 by Mary Jernigan

Printed in U.S.A.

Elle James, a *New York Times* bestselling author, started writing when her sister challenged her to write a romance novel. She has managed a full-time job and raised three wonderful children, and she and her husband even tried ranching exotic birds (ostriches, emus and rheas). Ask her, and she'll tell you what it's like to go toe-to-toe with an angry 350-pound bird! Elle loves to hear from fans at ellejames@earthlink.net or ellejames.com.

Books by Elle James

Harlequin Intrigue

Ballistic Cowboys

Hot Combat

SEAL of My Own

Navy SEAL Survival
Navy SEAL Captive
Navy SEAL to Die For
Navy SEAL Six Pack

Covert Cowboys, Inc.

Triggered
Taking Aim
Bodyguard Under Fire
Cowboy Resurrected
Navy SEAL Justice
Navy SEAL Newlywed
High Country Hideout
Clandestine Christmas

Visit the Author Profile page at
Harlequin.com for more titles.

CAST OF CHARACTERS

Jon "Ghost" Caspar—US Navy SEAL on loan to the Department of Homeland Security for Task Force Safe Haven, a special group of military men.

Charlie McClain—Telecommuting software engineer and part-time social-media analyst for Homeland Security. Lives with her daughter in Grizzly Pass, Wyoming.

Kevin Garner—Agent with the Department of Homeland Security in charge of Task Force Safe Haven.

Max "Caveman" Decker—US Army Delta Force soldier on loan to the Department of Homeland Security for Task Force Safe Haven.

"Hawkeye" Trace Walsh—US Army airborne ranger and expert sniper on loan to the Department of Homeland Security for Task Force Safe Haven.

Rex "T-Rex" Trainor—US Marine on loan to the Department of Homeland Security for Task Force Safe Haven.

Leroy Vanders—Rancher whose cattle herd was confiscated by the Bureau of Land Management because he refused to pay his fees for grazing his cattle on government property.

Tim Cramer—Pipeline inspector who lost his job when work dried up. With his marriage on the rocks and his wife threatening to take his child and move, he has nothing more to lose.

Bryson Rausch—Formerly the wealthiest resident of Grizzly Pass, who lost everything in the stock market.

Lolly McClain—Charlie McClain's six-year-old daughter.

Chapter One

Charlie McClain pinched the bridge of her nose and rubbed her eyes. Fifteen more minutes, and she'd call it a night. The computer screen was the only light shining in her house at eleven o'clock. She'd kissed her six-year-old daughter good-night nearly three hours ago, and made it a rule not to work past midnight. She was closing in on breaking that rule and knew she would pay for it in the morning.

She looked forward to the day when her student loans were paid off and a little money was socked away in the bank. Until then, she telecommuted developing software during the day and at night she moonlighted, earning additional money surfing the internet for the Department of Homeland Security.

Fortunately, she didn't have to use her own internet provider to do the DHS surfing. She lived on the edge of town, beside Grizzly Pass's small library with free Wi-Fi service.

Since she lived so close, she was able to tap in without any great difficulty. It had been one of the reasons she'd agreed to take on the task. As long as a hacker couldn't trace her searches back to her home address, she could surf with relative anonymity. She didn't know how sophisticated her targets were, but she didn't want to take any more chances than she had to. She refused to put her daughter at risk, should some terrorist she might root out decide to come after her.

Charlie had just about reached her limit when her search sent her to a social media group with some disturbing messages. The particular site was one the DHS had her monitor on a regular basis. Comprised of antigovernment supporters with axes to grind about local and national policy, it was cluttered with chatter tonight. The group called themselves Free America.

Charlie skimmed through the messages sent back and forth between the members of the group, searching for anything the DHS would be concerned about.

She'd just about decided there wasn't anything of interest when she found a conversation thread that made her page back to read through the entire communication.

Preparations are underway for TO of gov fac.

Citizen soldiers of WY be ready. Our time draws near.

A cold chill slid down Charlie's spine. TO could mean anything, but her gut told her TO stood for *takeover*. As a citizen of the US and the great state of Wyoming, she didn't like the idea of an anti-government revolt taking place anywhere in the United States, especially in her home state.

Granted, Wyoming stretched across hundreds of miles of prairie, rugged canyons and mountains. But there weren't that many large cities with government facilities providing prime targets. Cheyenne, the state capital, was on the other side of the state from where Charlie and her daughter lived.

Charlie backed up to earlier posts on the site. She needed to understand what their grievances were and maybe find a clue as to what government facility they were planning to take over. The more information she could provide, the more ammunition DHS would have to stop a full-scale attack. What government facility? What city? Who would be involved in the takeover? Hell, for that matter, what constituted a takeover?

Several of the members of the group complained about the government confiscating their cattle herds when they refused to pay the increase in fees for grazing rights on federal land. Others were angry that the oil pipeline work had been brought to a complete halt. They blamed the tree huggers and the politicians in Washington.

Still others posted links to gun dealer sites and local gun ranges providing training on tactical fire and maneuver techniques used by the military.

The more she dug, the less she liked what she was finding. So far, nothing indicated a specific date or location for the government facility takeover. Without hard facts, she wasn't sure she had anything to hand over to DHS. But her woman's intuition was telling her she had something here. She tried to follow the post back to its orgin, but didn't get very far.

A message popped up in Charlie's personal message box.

Who is this?

Shocked at being caught, Charlie lifted her hands off the computer keyboard.

I can see you. Come, pretty lady, tell me your name.

Charlie's breath lodged in her lungs. Could he see her? Her laptop had a built-in webcam. Had he hacked into it? She slammed the laptop shut and stared at the device as if it was a snake poised to bite. Her pulse raced and her hands shook.

Had he really seen her?

Pushing back her office chair, Charlie stood. If

he had seen her, so what? She could be anyone who just stumbled onto the site. No harm, no foul. She shoved a hand through her thick hair and walked out of her office and down the hallway to the little bedroom where her six-year-old daughter lay peacefully sleeping.

The message had shaken her and left her rethinking her promise to help DHS monitor for terrorists.

Charlie tucked the blankets up around her daughter's chin and straightened. She shouldn't let the message bother her. It wasn't as if just anyone could trace her efforts at snooping back to her laptop. To track her down would require the skills of a master hacker. And they'd only get as far as the library's free Wi-Fi.

Too wound up to sleep, Charlie walked around her small cottage, checking the locks on the windows and doors, wishing she had a big bruiser of a dog to protect her if someone was to breach the locks.

Charlie grabbed a piece of masking tape, opened the laptop and covered the lens of the webcam. Feeling a little better, she took a seat at her desk and drafted an email to Kevin Garner, her handler at DHS. She'd typed This might not be anything, but check it out. Then she went back to the social media site and was in the middle of copying the site's location URL where she'd found the damning call to arms when another message popped up on her screen.

You're trespassing on a private group. Cease and desist.

Charlie closed the message and went back to pasting the URL into her email.

Another message popped up.

I know what you look like and it won't take long to trace your location. Pass on any information from this group and we'll find you.

The next thing to pop up was an image of herself, staring down at her laptop.

A horrible feeling pooled in the pit of Charlie's belly. Could he find her? Would he really come after her?

Suddenly the dead bolt locks didn't seem to be enough protection against whoever was at the other end of the computer messaging.

Charlie grabbed her phone and dialed Kevin's number. Yeah, it was after eleven o'clock, but she needed to hear the sound of someone's voice.

"I got it," Kevin's wife, Misty, answered with a groggy voice. "Hello."

"Misty, it's Charlie."

"Charlie. Good to hear from you. But what time is it? Oh, my, it's almost midnight. Is anything wrong?"

Charlie hesitated, feeling foolish, but unwilling to end the call now. She squared her shoulders. "I need to talk to Kevin."

A moment later, Kevin's voice sounded in her ear. "Charlie, what's up?"

She drew in a deep breath and let it out, willing her voice to quit shaking as she relayed the information. "I was surfing the Free America social media site and found something. I'm not sure it's anything, but it set off alarm bells in my head."

"Shoot."

She told him about the message and waited for his response.

"Doesn't sound good. Got anything else?"

"I looked, but couldn't find anything detailing a specific location or government facility."

"I don't like it, but I can't get a search warrant if I don't have a name or location."

"That's what I figured, but that isn't all."

"What else have you got for me?"

"While I was searching through the social media site, a message popped up."

"A message?" he asked.

Charlie read the messages verbatim from her laptop. "He has my picture."

"Hmm. That he was able to determine you were

looking at the site and then able to take command of your laptop long enough to snap a picture has me concerned."

"You're not the only one." She scrubbed a hand down her face, tired, but too agitated to go to sleep. "I was using the library's Wi-Fi. He won't be able to trace back to my computer."

"That's good. More than likely he's near the state capital."

"Are you willing to bet your life on that?" she asked.

"My life, yes."

"What about the life of your son or daughter?" Charlie asked. She knew he had two kids, both under the age of four. "Would you be able to sleep knowing someone is threatening you? And by threatening you, they threaten your family."

"Look, can you make it through the night?" Kevin asked. "It'll be tomorrow before I can do anything."

"I'll manage."

"Do you want me to come over?"

She shook her head, then remembered she was on the phone. "No. I have a gun. I know how to use it. And I really don't think he'll trace me to my home address so quickly. We don't even know if he has that ability."

"He snapped a picture of you," Kevin reminded

her. "I'd say he's internet savvy and probably pretty good at hacking."

"Great." Charlie sighed. "I'll do okay tonight with my H&K .40 caliber pistol. But tomorrow, I might want some help protecting my daughter."

"On it. I'm expecting reinforcements this week. As soon as they arrive, I'll send someone over to assess the situation."

"Thanks." Charlie gripped the phone, not in a hurry to hang up. As if by so doing, she'd sever her contact permanently with the outside world and be exposed to the potential terrorist on the other end of the computer network.

"Look, Charlie, I can be there in fifteen minutes."

"No, really. I'll be fine." And she would be, as soon as she pulled herself together. "Sorry to bother you so late."

"Call me in the morning. Or call me anytime you need to," Kevin urged.

She ended the call and continued to hold the phone so tightly her fingers hurt.

What was supposed to have been an easy way to make a little extra cash had just become a problem. Or she was overreacting.

Just to be safe, she entered her bedroom and opened her nightstand where she kept the pistol her father had purchased for her when she'd graduated college. She could call her parents, but they were on a river cruise in Europe. Why bother them if this turned out to be nothing?

She found her pistol beneath a bottle of hand lotion and a romance novel. The safety lock was in place from the last time she'd taken it to Deputy Frazier's ranch for target practice six months ago. She removed the lock, dropped the magazine full of bullets and slid back the bolt. Everything appeared to be in working order. She released the bolt, slammed the magazine into the handle and left the lock on. She'd sleep in the lounge chair in the living room so that she would be ready for anything. She settled in the chair, her gun in her hand, hoping she didn't fall asleep, have a bad dream and shoot a hole in her leg.

She positioned herself in the chair, her gaze on the front door, her ears tuned in to the slightest sound. Not that she expected anyone to find her that night, but, if they did, she'd be ready.

JON "GHOST" CASPAR woke to the sun glaring through his windshield on its early morning rise from the horizon. He'd arrived in Grizzly Pass sometime around two o'clock. The town had so little to offer in the way of amenities, he didn't bother looking for a hotel, instead parking his truck in the empty parking lot of a small grocery store.

Not ten minutes after he'd reclined his seat and

closed his eyes, a sheriff's deputy had rolled up beside him and shone a flashlight through his window.

Ghost had sat up, rolled down his window and explained to the deputy he'd arrived later than he'd expected and would find a hotel the next day. He just needed a few hours of sleep.

The deputy had nodded, warned him not to do any monkey business and left him alone. To make certain Ghost didn't perform any unsavory acts, the deputy made it his sole mission to circle the parking lot every half hour like clockwork until shift change around six in the morning.

Ghost was too tired to care. He opened his eyes briefly for every pass, but dropped back into the troubled sleep of the recently reassigned.

He resented being shuffled off to Wyoming when he'd rather be back with his SEAL team. But if he had to spend his convalescence as a loaner to the Department of Homeland Security, it might as well be in his home state of Wyoming, and the hometown he hadn't visited in a long time.

Seven years had passed since the last time he'd come back. He didn't have much reason to return. His parents had moved to a Florida retirement community after his father had served as ranch foreman for a major cattle ranch for the better part of forty years. Ranching was a young man's work, hard on a body and unforgiving when it came to accidents.

The man deserved the life of leisure, soaking up the warm winter sunrays and playing golf to his heart's content.

Ghost adjusted his seat to the upright position and ran a hand through his hair. He needed a shower and a toothbrush. But a cup of coffee would have to do. He was supposed to report in to his contact, Kevin Garner, that morning to receive instructions. He hoped like hell he'd clarify just what would be entailed in the Safe Haven Task Force. To Ghost, it sounded like a quick path to boredom.

Ghost didn't do boredom well. It nearly got him kicked out of the Navy while in rehab in Bethesda, Maryland, at the Walter Reed National Military Medical Center. He was a SEAL, damn it. They had their own set of rules.

Not according to Joe, his physical therapist. He'd nearly come to blows with the man several times. Now that Ghost was back on his own feet without need of crutches, he regretted the idiot he'd been and had gone back to the therapy center to apologize.

Joe had laughed it off, saying he'd been threatened with far worse.

A smile curled Ghost's lips at the memory. Then the smile faded. He could get around without crutches or a cane, but the Navy hadn't seen fit to assign him back to his team at the Naval Special Warfare Group, or DEVGRU, in Virginia. Instead he'd been given Temporary Duty assignment in Wyoming, having been personally requested by a DHS task force leader.

What could possibly be so hot that a DHS task force leader could pull enough strings to get a highly trained Navy SEAL to play in his homeland security game? All Ghost could think was that man had some major strings to pull in DC. As soon as he met with the DHS guy, he hoped to make it clear he wanted off the assignment and back to his unit.

The sooner the better.

He'd left Grizzly Pass as a teen, fresh out of high school. Though his father loved the life of a ranch foreman, Ghost had wanted to get out of Wyoming and see the world. He'd returned several times, the last to help his parents pack up their things to move to Florida. He'd taken a month of leave to guide his parents through the biggest change in their lives and to say goodbye to his childhood home one last time.

With his parents leaving Wyoming, he had no reason to return. Having recently graduated from the Basic Underwater Demolition/SEAL training and having just completed his first deployment in his new role, Ghost was on a path to being exactly what he wanted—the best Navy SEAL he could be. A month on leave in Grizzly Pass reminded him why he couldn't live there anymore. At the same time, it reminded him of why he'd loved it so much.

He'd been home for two weeks when he'd run into a girl he'd known since grade school, one who'd been his friend through high school, whom he'd lost touch with when he'd joined the Navy. She'd been the tagalong friend he couldn't quite get rid of, who'd listened to all of his dreams and jokes. She was as quirky and lovable as her name, never asking anything of him but a chance to hang around.

With no intention of starting a lasting relationship, he'd asked her out. He'd told her up front he wasn't there to stay and he wouldn't be calling her after he left. She'd been okay with that, stating she had no intention of leaving Wyoming and she wouldn't be happy with a man who would be gone for eleven months of the year. But she wouldn't mind having someone to go out with while he was there.

No strings attached. No hearts broken.

Her words.

Looking back, Ghost realized those two weeks had been the best of his life. He'd recaptured the beauty of his home and his love of the mountains and prairies.

Charlie had taken him back to his old haunts in her Jeep, on horseback and on foot. They'd hiked, camped and explored everywhere they'd been as kids, topping it off by skinny-dipping in Bear Paw Creek.

That was when the magic multiplied exponentially. Their fun-loving romp as friends changed in an instant. Gone was the gangly girl with the braid hanging down her back. Naked, with nothing but the sun touching her pale skin, she'd walked into the water and changed his life forever.

He wondered if she still lived in Grizzly Pass. Hell, for the past seven years, he'd wanted to call her and ask her how she was doing and if she still thought about that incredible summer.

He supposed in the past seven years, she'd gone on to marry a local rancher and had two or three kids by now.

Ghost sighed. Since they'd made love in the fresh mountain air, he'd thought of her often. He still carried a picture of the two of them together. A shot his father had taken of them riding double on horse-back at the ranch. He remembered that day the most. That was the day they'd gone to the creek. The day they'd first made love. The first day of the last week of his leave.

Having just graduated from college, she'd started work with a small business in town. She worked half days and spent every hour she wasn't working with Ghost. When he worried about her lack of sleep, she'd laughed and said she could sleep when he was gone. She wanted to enjoy every minute she could with him. Again, no strings attached. No hearts broken.

Now, back in the same town, Ghost glanced

around the early morning streets. A couple of trucks rumbled past the grocery parking lot and stopped at the local diner, pulling in between several other weathered ranch trucks.

Apparently the food was still good there.

A Jeep zipped into the diner's parking lot and parked between two of the trucks.

As his gaze fixed on the driver's door as it opened, Ghost's heartbeat stuttered, stopped and raced on.

A man in dark jeans and a dark polo shirt climbed out and entered the diner.

His pulse slowing, Ghost let out a sigh, squared his shoulders and twisted the key in the ignition. He was there to work, not rekindle an old flame, not when he was going to meet a man about his new assignment and promptly ask to be released to go back to his unit. The diner was the designated meeting place and it was nearing seven o'clock—the hour they'd agreed on.

Feeling grungy and road-weary, Ghost promised himself he'd find a hotel for a shower, catch some real sleep and then drive back to Virginia over the next couple of days.

He drove out of the parking lot and onto Main Street. He could have walked to the diner, but he wanted to leave straight from there to find that hotel and the shower he so desperately needed. Thirty minutes max before he could leave and get some rest.

Ghost parked in an empty space in the lot, cut the engine, climbed out of his truck and nearly crumpled to the ground before he got his leg straight. Pain shot through his thigh and kneecap. The therapist said that would happen if he didn't keep it moving. After his marathon drive from Virginia to Wyoming in under two days, what did he expect? He held on to the door until the pain subsided and his leg straightened to the point it could hold his weight.

Once he was confident he wouldn't fall flat on his face, he closed the truck door and walked slowly into the diner, trying hard not to limp. Even the DHS wouldn't want a man who couldn't go the distance because of an injury. Not that he wanted to keep the job with DHS. No. He wanted to be back with his unit. The sooner the better. They'd get him in shape better than any physical therapist. The competition and camaraderie kept them going and made them better, stronger men.

Once inside the diner, he glanced around at the men seated at the tables. Most wore jeans and cowboy boots. Their faces were deeply tanned and leathery from years of riding the range in all sorts of weather.

One man stood out among the others. He was tall and broad-shouldered, certainly capable of hard work, but his jeans and cowboy boots appeared new. His face, though tanned, wasn't rugged or hardened by the elements. He sat in a corner booth, his gaze narrowing on Ghost.

Figuring the guy was the one who didn't belong, Ghost ambled toward him. "DHS?" he asked, his tone low, barely carrying to the next booth.

The man stood and held out his hand. "Kevin Garner. You must be Jon Caspar."

Ghost shook the man's hand. "Most folks call me Ghost."

"Nice to meet you, Ghost." Garner had a firm grip, belying his fresh-from-the-Western-store look. "Have a seat."

Not really wanting to stay, Ghost took the chair indicated.

The DHS man remained standing long enough to wave to a waitress. Once he got her attention, he sat opposite Ghost.

On close inspection, his contact appeared to be in his early thirties, trim and fit. "I was expecting someone older," Ghost commented.

Garner snorted. "Trust me, I get a lot of push-back for what I'm attempting. Most think I'm too young and inexperienced to lead this effort."

Ghost leaned back in his seat and crossed his arms over his chest. "And just what effort is that?"

Before the DHS representative could respond, the waitress arrived bearing a pot of coffee and an empty mug. She poured a cup and slapped a laminated menu on the table. "I'll be back."

As soon as she left, Garner leaned forward, resting his elbows on the table. "Safe Haven Task Force was my idea. If it works, great. If it fails, I'll be looking for another job. I'm just lucky they gave me a chance to experiment."

"Frankly, I'm not much on experiments, but I'll give you the benefit of a doubt. What's the experiment?"

"The team you will be part of will consist of some of the best of the best from whatever branch of service. They will be the best tacticians, the most skilled snipers and the smartest men our military has produced."

"Sorry." Ghost shook his head. "How do I fit into that team?"

Garner slid a file across the table and opened it to display a dossier on Ghost.

Ghost frowned. SEALs kept a low profile, their records available to only a very few. "How did you get that file?"

He sat back, his lips forming a hint of a smile. "I asked for it."

"Who the hell are you? Better still, what politician is in your pocket to pull me out of my unit for this boondoggle gig?" Ghost leaned toward Garner, anger simmering barely below the surface. "Look, I didn't ask for this assignment. I don't even want to be here. I have a job with the Navy. I don't need this."

Garner's eyes narrowed into slits. "Like it or not, you're on loan to me until I can prove out my theory. Call it a Temporary Duty assignment. I don't care what you call it. I just need you until I don't need you anymore."

"There are much bigger fish to fry in the world than in Grizzly Pass, Wyoming."

"Are you sure of that?" Garner's brow rose. "While you and your teammates are out fighting on foreign soil, we've had a few homegrown terrorists surface. Is fighting on foreign soil more important than defending your home turf?"

"I might fall for your line of reasoning if we were in New York, or DC." Ghost shook his head. "We're in Grizzly Pass. We're far away from politicians, presidents and wealthy billionaires. We're in the backside of the backwoods. What could possibly be of interest here?"

"You realize there's a significant amount of oil running through this state at any given time. Not to mention, it's also the state with the most active volcano."

"Not buying it." Ghost sat back again, unimpressed. "It would take a hell of an explosion to get things stirred up with the volcano at Yellowstone."

"Well, this area is a hotbed for antigovernment movements. There are enough weapons being stashed and men being trained to form a sizable army. And we're getting chatter on the social media sites indicating something's about to go down."

"Can you be more specific?"

Garner sighed. "Unfortunately, not yet."

"If you're done speculating, I have a two-day drive ahead of me to get back to my unit." Ghost started to rise, but the waitress arrived at that time, blocking his exit from the booth.

"Are you ready to order?"

"I'm not hungry."

Garner gave the waitress a tight smile. "I'd like the Cowboy Special, Marta."

Marta faced Ghost. "It's not too late to change your mind."

"The coffee will hold me." Until he could get to Cheyenne where he'd stop for food.

After Marta left, Garner leaned toward Ghost. "Give me a week. That's all I ask. One week. If you think we're still tilting at windmills, you can go back to your unit."

"How did I get the privilege of being your star guinea pig?"

Garner's face turned a ruddy shade of red and he pressed his lips together. "I got you because you weren't cleared for active duty." He raised his hand.

"Don't get me wrong. You have a remarkable record and I would have chosen you anyway, once you'd fully recovered."

That hurt. The Navy had thrown the DHS a bone by sending a Navy SEAL with a bummed-up leg. Great. So they didn't think he was ready to return to duty either. The anger surged inside him, making him mad enough to prove them wrong. "All right. I'll give you a week. If we can't prove your theory about something about to go down, I'm heading back to Virginia."

Garner let out a long breath. "That's all I can ask."

Ghost smacked his hand on the table. "So, what exactly am I supposed to do?"

"One of our operatives was threatened last night. I need you to work with her while she tries to figure out who exactly it is and why they would feel the need to harass her." He handed Ghost his business card, flipping it over to the backside where he'd written an address. "This is her home address here in Grizzly Pass."

"I know where that is." Orva Davis lived there back when he was a kid. She used to chase the kids out of her yard, waving a switch. She'd been ancient back then, she couldn't possibly be alive now. "She's expecting me this morning?"

"She'll be happy to see anyone this morning. The sooner the better."

"Who is she?"

At that exact moment Garner's cell phone buzzed. He glanced down at the caller ID, his brows pulling together. "Sorry, I have to take this. If you have any questions, you can call me at the number on the front of that card." He pushed to his feet and walked out of the building, pressing the phone to his ear.

After tossing back the last of his coffee, Ghost pulled a couple of bills from his wallet and laid them on the table. He took the card and left, passing Garner on his way to his truck.

The DHS man was deep in conversation, turned completely away from Ghost.

Ghost shrugged. He'd had enough time off that he was feeling next to useless and antsy. But he could handle one more week. He might even get in some fly-fishing.

He slid behind the wheel of his pickup and glanced down at the address. Old Orva Davis couldn't possibly still be alive, could she? If not her, who was the woman who'd felt threatened in this backwater town? Probably some nervous Nellie.

He'd find out soon enough.

And then…one week.

Chapter Two

Charlie had nodded off once or twice during the night, waking with a jerk every time. Thankfully, she hadn't pulled the trigger and blown a hole in the door, her leg or her foot.

She was up and doing laundry when Lolly padded barefoot out of her bedroom, dragging her giant teddy bear. "I'm hungry."

"Waffles or cereal?" Charlie asked, forcing a cheerful smile to her tired face.

"Waffles," Lolly said. "With blueberry syrup."

"I'll start cooking, while you get dressed." Charlie plugged in her waffle iron, mixed the batter and had a waffle cooking in no time. She cleaned off the small dinette table that looked like a throwback to the fifties, with its speckled Formica top and chrome legs. In actuality, the table did date back to the fifties. It was one of the items of furniture that had come with the house when she'd bought it. She'd been fortunate enough to find the bright red vinyl fabric to recover the seats, making them look like new.

On a tight budget, with only one income-producing person in the family, a car payment and student loans to pay, she couldn't afford to be extravagant.

She was rinsing fresh blueberries in the sink when a dark figure suddenly appeared in the window in front of her. Charlie jumped, her heart knocking against her ribs. She laughed when she realized it was Shadow, the stray she and Lolly had fed through the winter. Charlie was far too jumpy that morning. The messages from the night before were probably all bluster, no substance, and she'd wasted a night she could have been sleeping, worrying about nothing.

The cat rubbed her fur against the window screen. When that didn't get enough attention, she stretched out her claws and sank them into the screen netting.

"Hey! Get down." Charlie tapped her knuckles against the glass and the cat jumped down from the ledge. "Lolly! Shadow's hungry and my hands are full."

Lolly entered the room dressed in jeans, a pink T-shirt and the pink cowboy boots she loved so much. The boots had been a great find on one of their rare trips to the thrift shop in Bozeman, Montana. "I'll get the bowl." She started for the back door.

I'll find you.

The message echoed in Charlie's head and she dropped the strainer of blueberries into the sink and hurried toward her daughter. "Wait, Lolly. I'll get the cat bowl. Tell you what, you grab a brush, and we'll braid your hair this morning."

Charlie waited until her daughter had left the kitchen, then she unlocked the dead bolt and glanced out at the fresh green landscape of early summer in the Rockies. The sun rose in the east and a few puffy clouds skittered across the sky. Snow still capped the higher peaks in stunning contrast to the lush greenery. How could anything be wrong on such a beautiful day?

A loud ringing made her jump and then grab for the telephone mounted on the wall beside her.

"Hello," she said, her voice cracking, her body trembling from being startled.

"Charlie, it's me, Kevin."

"Thank goodness." She laughed, the sound even shakier than her knees.

"Any more trouble last night?"

She shook her head and then remembered he couldn't see her. "No. I'm beginning to think I'm paranoid."

"Not at all. In fact, I'm sending someone over to check things out. He should be there in a few minutes."

"Oh. Okay. Thanks, Kevin."

"The guy I'm sending is one hundred percent trustworthy. I'd only send the best to you and Lolly." He broke off suddenly. "Sorry. I have an incoming call. We'll talk later."

"Thanks, Kevin." Feeling only slightly better, Charlie returned the phone to its charger and stepped out onto the porch.

Shadow rubbed against her legs and trotted to the empty bowl on the back porch steps.

"Impatient, are we?" Charlie walked out onto the porch, shaking off the feeling of being watched, calling herself all kinds of a fool for being so paranoid. She dropped to her haunches to rub the cat behind the ears.

Shadow nipped at her fingers, preferring food to fondling. Charlie smiled. "Greedy thing." She bent to grab the dish. When she rose, she caught movement in the corner of her eyes and then there were jean-clad legs standing in front of her.

She gasped and backed up so fast, she forgot she was still squatting and fell on her bottom. A scream lodged in her throat and she couldn't get a sound to emerge.

The man looming over her was huge. He stood with his back to the sun, his face in the shadows, and he had hands big enough to snap her bones like twigs. He extended one of those hands.

Charlie slapped it away and crab-walked backward toward the door. "Wh-who are you? What do you want?" she whispered, her gaze darting to the left and the right, searching for anything she could use as a weapon.

"Geez, Charlie, you'd think you'd remember me." He climbed the steps and, for the second time, reached for her hand. Before she could jerk hers away, he yanked her to her feet. A little harder than either of them expected.

Charlie slammed against a wall of muscle, the air knocked from her chest. Or had her lungs seized at his words? She knew that voice. Her pulse pounded against her eardrums, making it difficult for her to hear. "Jon?"

He brushed a strand of her hair from her face. "Hey, Charlie, I didn't know you were my assignment." He chuckled, that low, sexy sound that made her knees melt like butter.

Her heart burst with joy. He'd come back. Then as quickly as her joy spread, anger and fear followed. She flattened her palms against his chest and pushed herself far enough way, Jon was forced to drop his hands from around her waist. "What are you doing here?" she demanded.

"I'm on assignment." He grinned. "And it appears you're it."

She shook her head. "I don't understand."

"Kevin Garner sent me. The Navy loaned me to

the Department of Homeland Security for a special task force. I thought it was going to be a boondoggle, and actually asked to be released from the assignment. But it looks like it won't be nearly as bad as I'd anticipated."

Charlie straightened her shirt, her heartbeat hammering, her ears perked to the sound of little footsteps. "You were right. Get Kevin to release you. Go back to the Navy. They need you more there."

"Whoa. Wait a minute. I promised Kevin I'd give it a week." Jon gripped her arms. "Why the hurry to get rid of me? As I recall, we used to have chemistry."

She shrugged off his hand. "That was a long time ago. A lot has changed since then. Please. Just go. I can handle the situation myself."

"If you're in trouble, let me help."

"No." God, why did he have to come back now? And why was it so hard to get rid of him? He'd certainly left without a care, never looking back or contacting her. Well, he could stay gone, for all she gave a damn. "I'm pretty sure I don't need you. Ask Kevin to assign you elsewhere."

"Mommy, I found the brush." Lolly pushed through the back door, waving a purple-handled hairbrush. "You can braid my hair now." Charlie's daughter, with her clear blue eyes and fiery auburn hair tumbling down her back, stepped through the door and stopped. Her mouth dropped open and her head tilted way back as she stared up at the big man standing on her porch. "Mommy?" she whispered. "Who is the big man?"

Charlie's heart tightened in her chest. If only her daughter knew. But she couldn't tell her and she couldn't tell Jon. Not after all these years. Not when he'd be gone again as soon as he could get Kevin to release him. "This is Mr. Caspar. He was just leaving." Thankfully, her daughter looked like a miniature replica of herself, but for the eyes. No one had guessed who the father was, except for her parents, and they'd been very discreet about the knowledge, never throwing it up in her face or giving her a hard time for sleeping with him without a wedding ring.

Jon dropped to his haunches and held out his hand. "Would you like for me to brush your hair? I used to do it for your mother."

The memory of Jon brushing the hay and tangles out of her hair brought back a rush of memories Charlie would rather not have resurrected. Not now. Not when it had taken seven years to push those memories to the back of her mind. She had too much at stake.

Charlie laid a hand on her daughter's shoulder. "Mr. Caspar was leaving."

He shook his head and crossed his arms over his chest. "Sorry. I promised to stay for a week. I don't go back on my word."

No, he didn't. He'd told her he wasn't looking for a long-term relationship when he'd last been in town. He'd lived up to his word then, leaving without once looking back. "Well, you'll have to keep your promise somewhere else besides my back porch."

Her daughter tugged on the hem of her T-shirt. "Mommy, are you mad at the man?"

With a sigh, Charlie shook her head. "No, sweetie, I'm not mad at him." Well, maybe a little angry that he'd bothered to come back after seven years. Or more that he'd waited seven years to return. Hell, she didn't know what to feel. Her emotions seemed to be out of control at the moment, bouncing between happiness at seeing him again and terror that he would discover her secret.

Since Jon seemed in no hurry to leave, she'd have to get tougher. Charlie turned her little girl and gave her a nudge toward the door. "Go back inside, Lolly. We adults need to have a talk."

Lolly grabbed her hand and clung to it. "I don't want to go." She frowned at Jon. "What if the big man hurts you?"

Lord, he'd already done that by breaking her heart. How could he hurt her worse?

GHOST WATCHED AS the little girl, who looked so much like her mother that it made his chest hurt, turned and entered the house, the screen door closing behind her.

Charlie hadn't waited around for him to come back. She'd gone on with her life, had a kid and probably had a husband lurking around somewhere. "Are you married?" He glanced over her shoulder, trying to see through the screen of the back door.

"Since you're not staying, does it matter?" She walked past him and down the stairs, grabbed a bowl from the ground and nearly tripped over a dark gray cat twisting around her ankles.

When Charlie stepped over the animal and started up the steps, the feline ran ahead and stopped in front of Ghost. She touched her nose to his leg as if testing him.

Ghost grew up on a ranch with barn cats. His father made sure they had two or three at any given time, but had them spayed and neutered to keep from populating the countryside with too many feral animals with the potential for carrying disease or rabies around the family and livestock.

He bent to let the cat sniff his hand and then scratched the animal's neck. "You didn't answer my question," he said. Why would she avoid the simple yes or no question?

"I don't feel like I owe you an explanation for what I've been doing for the past seven years." Her tone was tight, her shoulders stiff.

When he'd first seen her on the deck, he hadn't immediately recognized her. Her hair was longer and loose around her shoulders. When they'd been together, all those years ago, she'd worn her hair in a perpetual braid to keep it out of her face.

Her hips and breasts were fuller, even more enticing than before. Motherhood suited her. If possible, she was more beautiful and sexier than ever.

His gut twisted. But who was the father? Lolly was small. Maybe five? Though he didn't have a claim on Charlie, he never could stomach the idea of another man touching her the way he'd touched her.

The fact was babies didn't come from storks. So Charlie wasn't the open, straightforward woman she'd been all those years ago. She probably had a reason for being more reserved. Having a child might have factored into her current stance.

He straightened. "So, tell me about the threats."

"You're not going away, are you?" Her brows drew together, the lines a little deeper than when she'd been twenty-two. She sighed. "I really wish you would just go. I have enough going on."

"Without me getting in the way?" He shook his head. "I'm only going to be here a week. Unless you have a husband who is willing to take care of you, let me help you and your family for the week." He smiled, hoping to ease the frown from her brow.

"Show me a husband and I'll leave." He cocked his brows.

She stared at him for a long, and what appeared to be wary, moment before she shook her head. "There isn't a husband to take care of us."

"Is he out of town?" He wasn't going to let it go. The thought of Charlie and her little girl being threatened didn't sit well with him. Who would do that to a lone woman and child? "I could stay until he returns."

"I told you. There isn't a husband. Never has been."

He couldn't help a little thrill at the news. But if no husband, who was the jerk who'd gotten her pregnant and left her to raise the child alone?

His heart stood still and his breath lodged in his lungs. Everything around him seemed to freeze. *No. It couldn't be.* "How old is Lolly?"

"Does it matter?" Charlie spun and walked toward the door. "If you want to see the threats, follow me."

He caught her arm and pulled her around to face him, his fingers digging into her skin. "How old is she?" he demanded, his lips tight, a thousand thoughts spinning in his head, zeroing in on one.

For a long moment, she met his gaze, refusing to back down. Finally, she tilted her chin upward a fraction and answered, "Six."

"Just six?" His gut clenched.

"Six and a few months."

Her words hit him like a punch in the gut. Ghost fought to remain upright when he wanted to double over with the impact. Instead, he dropped his hands to his sides and balled his fists. "Is she—"

"Yours?" She shrugged. "Does it matter? Will it change anything?"

"My God, Charlie!" He grabbed her arms wanting to shake her like a rag doll. But he didn't. "I have a daughter, and you never told me?"

"You were going places. You had a plan, and a family wasn't part of it. What did you expect me to do? Get an abortion? Give her up for adoption?"

"Hell, no." He choked on the words and shoved a hand through his hair. "I can't believe it." His knees wobbled and his eyes stung.

He turned toward the back door. The little auburn-haired girl-child stood watching them, her features muted by the screen.

That little human with the beautiful red hair, curling around her face was his daughter.

Chapter Three

Charlie walked toward the house. As she reached for the doorknob, her hands shook. Now that Jon knew about his daughter, what would he do? Would he fight for custody? Would he take her away for long periods of time? Would he hate her forever for keeping Lolly from him?

Questions spiraled out of control in Charlie's mind.

Lolly stood in the doorway, watching the two adults. Had she heard what had passed between them? Did she now know the big man was her father?

Up until Lolly had started school, she hadn't asked why she didn't have a father. Her world had revolved around Charlie. She didn't know enough about having a father to miss it.

Charlie pulled open the screen door, gathered her daughter in her arms and lifted her. "Hey, sweetie. Do you still have that brush?"

Her daughter held up the brush. "Is the big man going to stay?" She shot a glare at Jon. "I don't like him."

"Oh, baby, he's a nice man. How can you say you don't like him when you don't know him yet?"

That stubborn frown that reminded Charlie so much of Jon grew deeper. "I don't want to know him."

Charlie cringed and shot a glance over her shoulder at the father of her child. Had she been wrong to keep news of his daughter from him? Would he have wanted to be a part of her life from birth?

Jon's expression was inscrutable. If he was angry, he wasn't showing it. If Lolly's words hurt…again, he wasn't letting on.

Then he smiled. Though the effort appeared forced to Charlie, it had no less of an impact on her. She remembered how he'd smiled and laughed and played with her when he'd been there seven years ago.

She still had a picture they'd taken together. He'd been laughing at something she said when she'd snapped the photo of them together.

Her heart pinched in her chest. No matter how much she might want it, they couldn't go back in time. What they had was gone. They had to move on with their lives. How Jon would fit into Lolly's world had yet to be determined, if he chose to see her again. Now that Jon knew about her, Charlie couldn't keep him from being with her. She just hoped he didn't break Lolly's heart like he'd broken Charlie's all those years ago.

"Lolly, Mr. Caspar is going to be visiting for the next week. I think you'll like him." She stared into her daughter's eyes. "Please, give him a chance."

Lolly stared over Charlie's shoulder at the man standing behind her. She didn't say anything for a few seconds and then nodded. "Okay." Then she extended the hand with the brush toward Jon. "You can brush my hair."

A burst of laughter erupted from Charlie. She clapped her hand over her mouth, realizing it sounded more hysterical than filled with humor. Trust her daughter to put the man to the test first thing.

Charlie set her daughter on her feet.

Jon nodded, his face set, his gaze connecting with Lolly's. "I'd be honored." He took the brush from her and glanced around.

"You can have a seat in the kitchen," Charlie said. "I'll make some coffee. Have you had breakfast? I'm making blueberry waffles."

She went through the motions of being a good hostess when all she wanted to do was run out of the room screaming, lock herself in her room and cry until she had no more tears left. With a daughter watching her every move, Charlie couldn't give in to hysterics.

She'd cried more than enough tears over this man. No longer a young woman on the verge of life, she was a mother with responsibilities. Her number one priority was the well-being of her little girl.

Charlie rinsed the bowl in the sink, poured cat food into it and set it aside. Shadow jumped into the window again, startling her. "Cat, you're going to give me a heart attack," she muttered. "I'll be back."

As she left the kitchen with the cat food, she watched Jon and Lolly.

Jon had taken a seat at the kitchen table and stood Lolly with her back to him between his knees.

Charlie swallowed hard on the lump forming in her throat.

The Navy SEAL, with his broad shoulders and rugged good looks, eased the brush through Lolly's hair with a gentleness no one would expect from a man conditioned for combat.

Once outside, Charlie stood for a moment on the porch, reminding herself how to breathe. What was happening? She didn't know which was worse, being threatened by a potential domestic terrorist, or facing the man she'd fallen so deeply in love with all those years ago. Her life couldn't be more of a mess.

An insistent pressure on her ankles brought her

out of her own overwhelming thoughts and back to a hungry cat, purring at her feet.

"Sorry, Shadow. I keep forgetting that I'm not the only one in this world." She set the bowl on the porch, straightened and was about to turn when she saw movement in the brush near the edge of the tree line behind her house.

Narrowing her eyes, she stared into the shadows. Sometimes deer and coyotes made their way into her backyard. An occasional black bear wandered into town, causing a little excitement among residents. Nothing emerged and nothing stirred. Yet awareness rippled across her skin, raising gooseflesh.

Charlie rubbed her hands over her arms, the chill she felt having nothing to do with the temperature of the mountain air. She retreated behind the screen door where she stood just out of view from an outside observer. A minute passed, then another.

A rabbit hopped out of the shadows and sniffed the air, then bent to nibble on the clover.

Releasing the breath she'd been holding, Charlie turned toward the kitchen. Out of the corner of her eye, she saw the rabbit dart across the yard, away from the underbrush of the tree line.

Charlie shook off that creepy feeling and told herself not to be paranoid. Just because someone threatened her on the internet didn't mean someone would follow through on his threat.

She closed the back door and twisted the dead bolt. It didn't hurt to be careful. Walking back into the kitchen, she couldn't help feeling safer with Jon there. He had Lolly's hair brushed and braided into two matching plaits.

Her daughter leaned against Jon's knee, showing him her favorite doll.

Jon glanced up, his eyes narrowing slightly.

Oh, yeah. He was angry.

Charlie didn't doubt in the least he'd have a few choice words for her when Lolly wasn't in the room. And he had every right to be mad. He'd missed the first six years of his daughter's life.

Glad she had a bit of respite from a much-deserved verbal flogging, Charlie rescued a waffle from burning, poured batter into the iron and mixed up more in order to make enough for a grown man. Flavorful scents filled the air as the waffles rose.

Milking the excuse of giving her full attention to the production of the waffles, Charlie kept her back to Lolly and Jon. Yes, she was avoiding looking at Jon, afraid he'd see in her gaze that she wasn't totally over him. Afraid he'd aim that accusing glance at her and she'd feel even worse than she already did about not telling him.

"Here. Let me." A hand curled around hers and removed the fork from her fingers. "You're burning the waffles."

Charlie couldn't move—couldn't breathe. Jon stood so close he almost touched her. If she backed even a fraction of a step, her body would press against his.

God, she could smell that all too familiar scent that belonged to Jon, and only Jon—that outdoorsy, fresh mountain scent. She closed her eyes and swayed, bumping her back into his chest.

With his empty hand, he gripped her elbow, steadying her. Then he reached around her with the fork, opened the waffle iron and lifted out a perfect waffle. "Plates?" he said.

His mouth was so close to her ear, she could feel the warmth of his breath, causing uncontrollable shivers to skitter across her body.

Plates. Oh, yeah. She reached up to her right and started to pluck two plates from a cabinet. Then she remembered there were three of them now. After setting the plates on the counter, she turned away from the stove, desperate to put distance between her and Jon. Her body was on fire, her senses on alert for even the slightest of touches.

"Come on, Lolly, let's set the table while Mr. Caspar cooks." She grabbed the plates and started around Jon.

He shifted, blocking her path. "We *will* talk."

She stared at his chest, refusing to make eye contact. "Of course."

He stepped aside, allowing her to pass.

Charlie wanted to run from the room, but she knew she couldn't. Her daughter was a very observant child. She'd already figured out something wasn't right between her and Jon. Besides, running away would solve nothing.

Lolly gathered flatware from the drawer beside the sink.

Charlie set the plates on the table and went back to the cabinets for glasses. While she filled them with orange juice, she took the opportunity to study Jon while his back was to her.

The Navy SEALs had shaped him into even more of a man than he'd been before. His body was a finely honed weapon, his bulging muscles rippling with every movement. He'd been in great shape when he'd come home on leave seven years ago, but he was somehow more rugged, with a few new tattoos and scars on his exposed surfaces.

Charlie yearned to go to him, slip her arms around his waist and lean her cheek against his back like she had those weeks they'd been together. She longed to explore the new scars and tattoos, running her fingers across every inch of him.

He slipped waffles onto a platter and turned toward her, catching her gaze before she could look away.

Charlie froze, her eyes widening. Shoot, he'd

caught her staring. Could he see the longing in her eyes?

She dragged her gaze away and darted for the stove and the pan of blueberry syrup simmering on the back burner. Her hand trembled as she poured the hot syrup into a small pitcher.

"Careful, you might get burned." Jon took the pan from her and set it on the stove.

You're telling me? She'd been burned by him before. She had no intention of falling for him again. Her life was hectic enough as a single parent trying to make a living in a small town.

She hurried away from Jon and set the syrup in front of her daughter.

Lolly pointed to the end of the table. "Mr. Caspar, you can sit there." She climbed into her chair and waited for the adults to take their seats.

Charlie felt like she and Jon were two predatory cats circling the kill. She eased into her chair, her knees bent, ready to launch if things got too intense.

Jon frowned. "Are you sure you don't want your mother to sit here?"

Lolly shook her head. "She always sits across from me so we can talk."

Jon glanced at Charlie.

Charlie gave half of a smile. "That's the way we roll."

"Before we got our house, we sat on the couch to eat," Lolly offered.

"How long have you been in your house?" Jon asked.

"We moved in on my birthday." Lolly grinned. "I had my first birthday party here."

"What a special way to celebrate." Jon reached for the syrup and poured it over his stack of waffles. "Where did you live before?"

Charlie tensed.

Lolly shrugged. "Somewhere else." Her face brightened. "Did you know mommies go to school, too?"

Jon smiled. "Is that so?"

Lolly nodded. "Mommy went to school."

His brows hiked as he glanced toward Charlie.

Heat rose up her cheeks. She didn't want to talk about herself. They didn't need to go into all the details of their lives for the past seven years.

Jon didn't need to know that the years before they'd moved into the little house in Grizzly Pass had been lean. Too many times, Charlie had skipped a meal to have enough money to feed Lolly and pay for the babysitter. Working as a waitress during the day kept a roof over their heads and school at night didn't leave much time for her to be with her daughter. But they'd made their time together special. Now that she worked from home, Charlie was making up for all the times she couldn't be home.

Her daughter shoved a bite of waffle into her mouth and sighed. "Mmm."

Charlie almost laughed at the pure satisfaction on Lolly's face. They hadn't always eaten this well, and it hadn't been that long since she'd landed a job paying enough money that she could afford to buy a small house in her hometown.

Jon took a bite of the waffle, closed his eyes and echoed Lolly's approval. "Mmm. Your mother makes good waffles."

"You helped," Lolly pointed out.

"So he did." Charlie pushed her food around on her plate, her stomach too knotted to handle anything. Not with Jon Caspar sitting at her table.

Hell, Jon Caspar, the man she'd dreamed about for years, was sitting at her table. She pushed her chair back. "If you'll excuse me, I just remembered something."

She took her plate to the sink and was about to scrape the waffles into the garbage disposal when Jon's voice spoke up. "If you aren't going to eat them, I will."

She stopped with her fork poised over the sink. Walking back to the table, she set her plate down beside Jon's and then ran from the room.

So, I'm a big fat chicken. Sue me.

In an attempt to take her mind off the man in the kitchen, Charlie entered the guest bedroom she'd converted into an office. A futon doubled as a couch and a guest bed. The small desk in the corner that she'd purchased from a resale shop was just the right size for her. She spent most of her day in her office, working for a software developer she'd interned with during the pursuit of her second degree in Information Systems.

The shiny new business degree she'd finished right before that summer with Jon had landed her nothing in the way of a decent job. She'd stayed in Grizzly Pass with her parents through Lolly's birth, making plans and taking online courses.

She'd moved to Bozeman to return to school for a degree in Information Systems, looking for skills that wouldn't require her to move to a big city to make a living. She'd chosen that degree because of the opportunities available to telecommute. It had been a terrific choice, giving her the flexibility she needed to raise Lolly where she wanted and provide the family support her daughter needed. She had no regrets over her decision and now had the time to dedicate to her work and her small family of two.

She booted up her laptop and waited for the screen to come to life. As she waited, she glanced around the small room, wondering if Jon could fit his six-foot-three-inch frame on the futon. Ha! Fat chance. But he wasn't going to sleep in her room. Seven years apart changed everything.

Everything but the way her body reacted to his nearness.

Hell, he'd probably had a dozen other women.

Her heart stopped for a moment as another thought occurred. An image of Jon standing beside a woman wearing a wedding dress popped into her head and a led weight settled in her belly. He might have a wife somewhere. He'd said he was there for only a week. He might have someone waiting for him back home.

And kids.

Charlie pressed her hand to her mouth, her heart aching for Lolly. How would she feel about sharing her father with other children? Would she get along with a stepmother?

Her eyes stung and her throat tightened. Lolly's life had just gotten a lot more complicated.

The screen on her laptop blinked to life. No sooner had she opened her browser than a message popped up on her screen.

You told.
Beware retribution.

"Damn." She shut the laptop and laid her head on top of it. If only wishing could fix everything, she'd wish her problems away.

"Are you okay?" A large hand descended on her shoulder.

For a moment Charlie let the warmth chase away the chill inside her. Jon had always had a knack for making everything all right. He would help her figure out this problem. In one week, they'd solve the mystery of who was threatening her and possibly a government facility in the state of Wyoming. Just one week. And then she could get back to life as usual.

Who was she kidding? Jon wouldn't leave for good. He'd be back. For Lolly.

Charlie shrugged Jon's hand off her shoulder and sat straight, opening her laptop again. "I've had another message." When the screen lit, she leaned back, allowing Jon to read the message.

"Do you think it's some kid yanking your chain?" Jon asked.

"I wish it was." Charlie pushed her hair back from her forehead. She clicked the keyboard until she found the URL she'd bookmarked and brought it up. Scrolling through the messages, she searched for the one that had started it all. She backed up through the messages from around the date and time the call to arms had been made. It was gone.

"What the hell?" Charlie scrolled farther back. "It was here last night."

"Whoever posted it could have come back in and erased the message."

Charlie snorted. "That's fine. I saved a screenshot, just in case." She pulled up the picture and sat back, giving Jon a moment to read and digest the words. "Do you think I was overreacting by reporting it to DHS?"

Jon shook his head. "With everything happening in the country and around the world, you can't be too cautious." He reached around her and brought up the social media site and scrolled through the messages again.

"Yesterday, there were a lot more messages expressing dissatisfaction with the way the government was handling the grazing rights and pipeline work."

"Apparently, someone scrubbed the messages. These all appear to be regular chatter."

Charlie sighed. "I'm beginning to think I imagined it."

"You did the right thing by alerting DHS." He straightened and crossed his arms over his chest. "Let them handle it. They have access to people who can trace sites like this back to the IP address."

The phone on her desk rang, making Charlie jump. She grabbed the receiver and hit the talk button. "Hello."

"Charlie, Kevin here. I take it you've met Ghost?"

"Ghost?" She glanced up at Jon.

He nodded and whispered, "My call sign."

Heat rose in her chest and up into her cheeks. "Yes, I've met him." She'd met him a long time ago, but she didn't want to go into the details with her DHS handler. Kevin wasn't from Grizzly Pass, and there were certain things he didn't need to know.

"Is he there now?" Kevin asked.

"Yes."

"Let me talk to him."

Charlie handed the phone to Jon. "It's Kevin."

Jon took the phone.

When their fingers touched, that same electric shock she'd experienced the first time he'd touched her shot up her arm and into her chest. She couldn't do this. Being close to him brought up all the same physical reactions she'd felt when she was a young and impressionable twenty-two-year-old.

She pushed back in her chair and rose, putting distance between them. It wasn't enough. Being in the same room as Jon, aka Ghost, made her ultra aware of him. She wasn't sure how long she could handle being this close and not touching him.

"GHOST HERE." HE HELD the receiver to his ear, unused to using landlines. But then cell phones were practically useless in the remote towns of Wyoming.

"The rest of the team has arrived. I'd like you to

meet them and talk through a game plan for the security of the area."

"I thought you wanted me to stay with Ms. Mc-
Clain."

"I wanted you to assess the situation and give me
feedback. I think she'll be okay in broad daylight.
For now, you need to come to my digs above the
Blue Moose Tavern and meet the rest of the men."

Ghost glanced at Charlie.

She paced the length of the small office, chew-
ing on her fingernail.

"I'll bring her and the child with me." His gaze
locked on her.

Charlie's head shot up and she met his glance
with a frown. "Wherever you're going, you'll have
to go by yourself. I had plans to take Lolly with me
to the grocery store and the library. You don't need
to come with me. We can take care of ourselves."

"Is that Charlie talking?" Kevin asked.

Ghost nodded. "It is."

"Tell her I only need you for about an hour. Then
she can have you back."

Ghost covered the mouthpiece with his hand.
"Garner said he only needs me for an hour. Are you
sure you and Lolly will be okay for that time?"

She nodded. "Nobody will attack us in broad daylight."

Ghost snorted. Too many people assumed that

same sentiment and were dead because of it. "Stay out of the open and report in every time you come and go from a location."

"I really think we might be paranoid, but okay." She raised her hands. "I'll stay out of the open, and I'll report my comings and goings." Charlie crossed her arms over her chest and tilted her head back. "Happy?"

"Not really," he said, his lips pressing together. "I'd rather drop you where you want to go and pick you up later."

Her lips pressed into a thin line.

Ghost decided it was better not to argue while Garner waited on the phone.

"Everything set?" Garner asked.

Ghost stared at Charlie, not sure he was happy with the arrangement, but Charlie wasn't budging. "Yes. I'll see you in twenty minutes. That will give me time to take a shower."

"Will do." Garner ended the call.

"I have to meet with DHS and the team Garner is assimilating. Are you sure you'll be okay?"

She gave a firm nod. "Positive."

How she could be so certain was unfathomable to Ghost. He wasn't sure *he* was okay. Being near Charlie brought back too many memories and a resurgence of the passion he'd felt for the woman seven years ago.

When he met with Garner, he'd have to tell him that he might not be the right man for the job. They had a huge conflict of interest. He and Charlie had slept together. Hell, they had a child together.

Tired and grungy, he couldn't think straight. "I need a shower."

"What do you want me to do about it?" She stood with her arms crossed, a semibelligerent frown on her face.

The corners of his lips twitched. Ghost stepped up to her and tipped her chin with his finger. "There was a time when you would have offered to shower with me."

"I was young and stupid."

He chuckled. "And you don't want to get stupid together? There's a lot to be said for being stupid. Especially when you do this—" Before he could talk sense into his own head, he bent and touched his lips to her forehead. "And this." He moved from her forehead to the tip of her nose.

She closed her eyes and her chest rose on a deep, indrawn breath. She unwound her arms and laid her hands on his chest.

At first he thought she would push away, but her fingers curled into his shirt, giving him just enough encouragement.

"And this." Ghost pressed his lips to hers, tasting what he'd missed for all those years, drinking in her sweetness. Sweet ecstasy, he couldn't get enough. He slid his hands to her lower back and pressed her closer. Why had he stayed away so long?

He skimmed the seam of her lips with his tongue. When she opened her mouth on a gasp, he dived in, caressing her tongue with his in a long, slick slide, reestablishing his claim on her mouth.

She felt different, her curves fuller, her arms stronger, her hair longer, but she was the same inside. This woman was the only one who'd stayed with him over the years, her image tucked in the recesses of his mind as he prepared for combat. She was the reason he'd dedicated his life to serving his country. To protect her and all the other people who depended on him to secure their freedom. He risked his life so that others could live free and safe.

For a long moment, he pushed every reason he'd had for leaving her out of his mind and reveled in the warm wetness of her kiss, the sweet taste of blueberry syrup on her lips and the heat of her body pressed to his. His groin tightened, the fly of his jeans pressing into her belly.

"Mommy?"

Ghost leaped back as if he'd been splashed with ice water.

"What do you need, Lolly?" Charlie pressed one hand to her swollen lips and the other smoothed her hair before she turned to face her daughter standing in the doorway.

"Why were you kissing Mr. Caspar?"

Ghost half turned away from the child, his lips twitching. He'd leave that answer for Charlie. Although, he'd like to know the answer to that question, too.

Chapter Four

"Sweetheart, let's get your shoes on. We're going to get groceries. After that, we're going to the library. So gather your books." Charlie didn't answer her daughter's question, choosing to hustle her daughter out of her office and away from the man who'd just kissed her socks off. She called over her shoulder, "Help yourself to the shower. There are towels in the linen closet and plenty of soap and shampoo."

Her lips tingled, and she could still taste the sweetness of his mouth. Dear, sweet heaven, how was she going to keep her hands off the man if he was around all the time?

She needed air. She needed space. What she wanted was another kiss just like that one. With her knees wobbling, Charlie left Lolly in her room and hurried into the master bedroom where the bed was still neatly made. She jammed her feet into her cowboy boots and yanked a brush through her hair, securing it at the nape of her neck in a ponytail. After checking that the safety switch was set on her handgun, she slid it into her purse, hooked the strap over her shoulder, braced herself and stepped into the hallway.

Thankfully, Jon wasn't anywhere in sight.

Charlie released the breath she'd held.

Lolly emerged from her room carrying a stack of children's books.

"Let's put those in a bag." She gathered the books and carried them back into Lolly's room where she found her book backpack and slid them inside.

Lolly slipped the backpack over her shoulders and led the way from the room.

She ran ahead to the living room.

Charlie shook her purse, listening for the jingle of keys. When she didn't hear it, she returned to her bedroom and grabbed them from the nightstand.

Hurrying into the hallway, with her head down, tucking the keys into her purse, she ran into a wall of muscles.

Big, coarse hands gripped her arms, steadying her.

"Are you all right?"

Hell no, she wasn't. Her pulse raced and she was out of breath before she'd even begun her day. "I'm fine," she said, studying her hands resting on his chest.

And boy, was he fine, too. Charlie couldn't help but stare at the expanse of skin peeking through his unbuttoned shirt. She remembered the smattering of hair on his chest and how she used to run her fingers through the curls. Her fingers curled into his skin, wanting to slide upward to test the springiness of those hairs.

"Are you ready?"

More than you'll ever know. Charlie shook herself and pushed way. "I'm taking my car since I have to stock up on groceries."

"I'll follow you there."

"No need. It's only a block from Kevin's office. If I run into any trouble, you won't be far away." She shook her head. "We'll be fine."

He stared at her for a long moment.

Charlie met his gaze and held it, refusing to back down. He'd been gone seven years. He couldn't just walk back into her life and take over.

"Okay." He started buttoning his shirt. "Let's go."

Charlie's glance dropped to where his fingers worked the buttons through the holes. Seven years ago, she would have helped him button up, and then undo them one at a time, kissing a path down his chest.

Ghost's fingers paused halfway up. "I remember, too," he said, his voice low and gravelly.

Shivers rippled through her body and Charlie

swayed toward him. Then she stopped, mentally pulled herself together and said, "I don't know what you're talking about. And I don't care. Let's go."

She pushed past him, her arm bumping into his, the jolt of electricity generated in that slight touch turning her knees to jelly.

The sooner she got away from him, the sooner she'd get her mind back. What was it about the man that scrambled her brain and left her defenseless against his magnetism?

Lolly stood by the door, her thumbs hooked through the straps of her backpack.

Charlie grabbed her hand and stepped out. She waited for Ghost to exit as well before she turned to lock the door. Her hand shook as she tried to slide the key into the dead bolt lock. She fumbled and dropped them to the porch.

Ghost scooped them up, locked the door and dropped the keys into her open palm. "You sure you don't want me to come with you?"

Lolly looked up, a happy smile on her face. "Could he, Mommy?"

"Sweetheart, Mr. Caspar has to go to a meeting."

Ghost touched his daughter's chin and gave her a brief smile. "I'll see you in about an hour."

"Mommy, can we get ice cream at the Blue Moose?"

"Why don't we get ice cream at the grocery store and bring it home to eat?"

"Okay." Lolly skipped down the steps toward the Jeep.

Charlie followed, not wanting to prolong her time or conversation with Ghost. The more she was with him, the more she wanted to be with him, and the harder it would be when he left again.

The drive to the grocery store took less than three minutes. She could have walked the five blocks, but she didn't want Lolly to be exposed to the nutcase who was threatening her. And carrying enough groceries for them for the week would be difficult, especially since she planned to purchase enough for Ghost, if he stayed for the full week. A man that big had to have an appetite to match. If it was anything like it had been when he'd gotten back from BUD/S training, he could put away some groceries.

He'd looked thin and a little gaunt after his SEAL training. She'd read about BUD/S to understand a little more of what he'd gone through. They'd put him through hell. And those who stuck it out came out tougher and ready to take on anything.

He'd been tired but exhilarated at making it through.

Now, he appeared more battle weary than anything. And he limped. Had he been injured? Charlie pressed a hand to her belly. The thought of Ghost going into battle, being shot at and explosions going off around him, made her stomach twist. When he'd left her, she'd done her best to push him as far to the back of her mind as she could. But she couldn't turn off the television when she'd seen reports of Navy SEALs dying in a helicopter crash or risking their lives to save hostages in Africa or some other place halfway around the world.

Now that he was back and larger than life, all those fears would be even harder to suppress.

DESPITE HER ASSURANCE they'd be all right, Ghost followed Charlie all the way to the grocery store in his truck. He waited in the parking lot until they were safely inside the store. Then he drove the additional block to the Blue Moose Tavern. As he pulled into a parking space on Main Street, a disturbance in front of the feed store two blocks down caught his attention.

He climbed out of his truck and studied the gathering crowd.

"Ghost, glad you could make it." Kevin Garner stepped out of the tavern, followed by three other men. He stuck out his hand.

Ghost shook it. "Charlie and Lolly are getting groceries. What's going on at the feed store?"

"Some of the local ranchers are gathering to protest the Bureau of Land Management's increase in fees for grazing livestock on government land."

He'd read about the issues the ranchers were having and how BLM had confiscated entire herds of cattle from ranchers who refused to pay the fees in protest.

As the crowd got louder, a van rolled into town with antennas attached to the top. A cameraman and reporter leaped out and positioned themselves with a view of the angry ranchers behind them.

"Is this part of the problem we're here to help with?" one of the men standing near Kevin asked. He stuck out his hand to Ghost. "Name's Max Decker. My Delta team calls me Caveman."

Ghost gripped the man's hand. "Jon Caspar. Navy SEAL. Call me Ghost."

The next man stepped up and gripped Ghost's hand. "Trace Walsh. Marine. Expert marksman, earned the nickname Hawkeye."

A tall man with a crooked nose stepped up. "Rex Trainor. Army Airborne Ranger. They call me T-Rex."

Kevin turned back to the group. "Now that you've all met, let's take it to the loft." He led the way up the stairs on the side of the tavern and entered a combination office-apartment.

Ghost followed and entered a large room with a fold-up table stretched across the center. A bank of computers stretched across one wall, the screens lit. A wiry young man sat in front of a keyboard, his gaze shifting between three monitors.

"That's Clive Jameson. We call him Hack. He's the brains behind the computer we're using to track movement and data."

"Movement of what?" Caveman asked.

"What data?" T-Rex stepped up behind Hack.

"Grab a seat, I'll explain." Garner waved his hand at the metal folding chairs leaning against the wall. "It's not the ideal location and can get pretty noisy on Friday and Saturday nights, but it gives me the space I need to run the operation."

"What operation?" Hawkeye asked.

Kevin pointed to a large monitor hung on the wall. "Hack, could you bring up the map?"

The computer guy behind them clicked several keys and a digital map came up on the monitor.

"This is the tristate area of Wyoming, Montana and Idaho. There's been a lot of rumbling going on for various reasons in the area. Between the pipeline layoffs and the cattle-grazing rights, things are getting pretty hot. We're afraid sleeper cells of terrorists are embedding in the groups and stirring them up even more and providing them with the funding and weaponry to create havoc."

"This is a hot area, anyway. Haven't there been rumblings from the Yellowstone Caldera?" T-Rex asked.

Garner nodded. "That's another reason why you four were brought into this effort. The scientists at the Yellowstone Volcano Observatory have been tracking specific trembles. They think there might be an eruption in the near future. They don't think it will be a catastrophic event, but it has generated a lot of interest and tourists are pouring into Yellowstone National Park."

"So, what specifically makes you think something big is about to happen?" Ghost asked.

"Last week, we had two men go missing from the BLM. They had been out riding four-wheelers in grizzly country near some of the park's active hot springs." Garner stared at each of the men, one at a time, then said, "They didn't come back.

"Because they were armed with GPS capability we were able to find their ATVs hidden in the brush near a particularly deadly spring. There was no sign of a bear attack, which was the rescue team's first inclination. But they did find a shoe near the spring and skid marks as if someone was either dragging or pushing a body toward the toxic water. If the BLM men found their way into that pool, either on their own, or by other more forceful means, there would be absolutely nothing left for a family member to claim. Their tissue and bones would have dissolved."

"The perfect place to hide the bodies," T-Rex said, his tone low, his eyes narrowed.

"Why bring in the military?" Ghost asked.

"DHS is spread thin, monitoring our boarders and

the entrance and exit points of airports and ports. We don't have the manpower to provide assistance to a potentially volatile situation here. And frankly, I don't think we have sufficient combat training as afforded to active duty military." Kevin lifted his chin, his chest swelling. "I do know what our country is capable of, and what the best of the best could do to help the situation. You see, I'm prior military. Eight years as a Black Hawk helicopter pilot. I ferried troops in and out of combat as a member of the 160th Night Stalkers."

Ghost sat back in his chair. "So you've seen as much battle as any one of us."

"Not as intensely as you four have. But I've seen what you can do when the time comes. You're smart and you act instinctively when you need to."

Hawkeye tapped his fingers on the table. "We've been fighting in a war environment. That's not what this is."

"No? You saw that mob out there. It could escalate into a shooting match in seconds."

"Still, it's not up to us to police civilians," Caveman said. "That's why we have law enforcement."

"The law enforcement is either tapped out or worse." Garner shook his head. "We think some might be working with the people stirring things up."

Ghost leaned forward. "What exactly are you asking us to do here?"

"I need you to do several things. We have hot spots in the tristate area." Garner pointed to the map. "One is a survivalist group on the edge of Yellowstone National Park. With all the tourists flooding the park, I'm afraid they'll use it as an excuse to stage something big. I need someone to get inside the group, spy and report back."

"I'll take that one." T-Rex raised his hand. "I can infiltrate the survivalists' group."

"All I'm looking for now is information. If they do anything, you are not to engage." One by one, Garner looked each man in the eye. "Repeat, you are not to engage."

Caveman scratched the back of his head, his brows twisting. "We're combat veterans. Why involve us if we're not to engage?"

"We want to reserve engagement until it's the last resort." The DHS task force leader placed both hands on the table and leaned toward the men. "Think of it as a reconnaissance mission. You infiltrate wherever I need you to go, assess the situation and report back."

Ghost studied Kevin, his gut telling him the man wasn't giving it to them straight. "What else are you not telling us?"

Kevin straightened, his eyes narrowing, his lips thinning into a thin line. "One of the folks we employ who monitors the internet for anything that could be construed as a potential attack, ran across a message last night. More or less, it was a call to arms to take over a government facility."

The Marine, Army Ranger and Delta Force man leaned forward.

Because he'd already heard this story, Ghost sat back in his chair and waited for the rest of whatever Kevin had to say.

"Where?" T-Rex asked.

"When?" Hawkeye wanted to know.

"We don't have that information. I need you all to keep an ear to the ground. If you hear anything, no matter how inconsequential it might sound, relay it to me."

Ghost shook his head. "The disappearing BLM men and a poorly worded message can't be all that has you calling in the cavalry. What else?"

Kevin met Ghost's gaze. "We've also been concerned about message traffic from some of the people we've been monitoring for the past six months. Men who are connected with ISIS. We intercepted a message we decoded indicating a weapons movement to this area. Enough guns and ammunition to stage a significant takeover of a state capital. Enough ammunition for a standoff. Or the murder of a great number of people."

Ghost's gut clenched. His daughter was in the area in question. If something went down, she could be caught in the cross fire. He'd just found his daughter. He'd be damned if he lost her so soon.

He couldn't wait to get out of the meeting and back to his family.

His family. Ha! If Charlie had her way, he wouldn't be anywhere near them. He'd just have to convince her she'd be better off with him sticking around.

Chapter Five

Once inside the grocery store, Charlie whirled the cart around the narrow aisles, hurrying through the tiny store, gathering only what she needed for the week. The shelves appeared barer than usual. When she got to the counter, Mrs. Penders, one of the owners of the mom-and-pop store checked her items.

"Why are the shelves so empty, Mrs. P?" Charlie asked, setting her items on the counter, one at a time. "Are you expecting a delivery today?"

She snorted and rang up a loaf of bread, the last one on the shelf. "I got a shipment this morning. We had a run on the store earlier. Did you see the crowd gathering in front of the feed store?"

She hadn't. Charlie had been more concerned about Ghost following her that she hadn't glanced farther down the street. "I'm sorry. I didn't see the crowd. What's going on?"

"A group of ranchers are taking a stand against the Bureau of Land Management over what they did."

"What did they do?"

"They confiscated half of LeRoy Vanders's herd. He refused to pay his fees for grazing rights on federal land in protest of the increase."

"Confiscated a herd of cattle?" Charlie set the jug of milk on the counter. "Can they do that?"

Mrs. Penders nodded. "Can and did. Got all the local ranchers up in arms. Sheriff's talking to them now out front of the feed store.

"I hear Jon Caspar is back in town." Mrs. Penders rang up the milk and slid it into a bag, before she raised her gaze to capture Charlie's. "You two were a thing way back in the day, weren't you?"

Charlie shrugged. "We dated."

"If he needs a place to stay, I have a room over my garage," the store owner offered.

"Mr. Caspar is staying with us." Lolly tugged on her mother's shirt. "Isn't he, Mommy?"

Heat filled Charlie's cheeks. "Just for the week while he's in town. Then he'll have to go back to his job with the Navy."

"Can't he stay forever?" Lolly asked. "I like the way he brushes my hair."

"We'll discuss this later," Charlie said, hurriedly placing the last items on the counter.

Mrs. Penders was one of the worst gossips in town.

By the time Charlie reached home, the older woman would have word spread across the county that Charlie and Ghost were shacking up. She wouldn't be surprised if she got a call from her parents all the way in Europe asking about the man sleeping in her little house.

Mrs. Penders gave her a total, Charlie paid and pushed the cart out into the parking lot. Lolly helped her load the items into the back of her Jeep.

As she pulled out of the parking lot of the store, she glanced down the street toward the feed store. Just as Mrs. Penders had said, a crowd gathered, some of the men raised their hands, shaking fists in the air.

"This can't be good," Charlie muttered, turning the opposite direction, heading for her little house on the edge of town. She passed the library.

"Aren't we going to the library?" Lolly asked.

"After we unload and put the groceries away. It won't take long, and we can walk next door."

"Okay." Lolly helped her unload the groceries, carrying in the lighter bags.

Charlie put away the items, grabbed her own bag of books and Lolly's backpack. "Let's go see Ms. Florence. She might have some new books for you today."

Grizzly Pass was a very small town, but the residents were proud of the little library they'd helped to fund. Rebecca Florence was the preacher's daughter, with a fresh degree in library science. A quiet soul, she'd returned to her hometown, glad to escape the hustle and bustle of Denver, where she'd attended her father's alma mater.

Happy to take over duties of town librarian from her aging mother, she slipped into the role with ease. Though shy and quiet, she managed to bring the library up to twenty-first century standards, writing for grant money to have computers installed and providing Wi-Fi internet for those who couldn't afford their own satellite internet.

Charlie enjoyed talking with Rebecca about the latest books. The woman was a wealth of knowledge and read extensively in fiction and nonfiction.

Before Charlie left the house, she placed a call to Kevin. His computer guy, Hack, answered the call. "He stepped out front. Is this an emergency? Do you want me to run out and catch him?"

"No. Just have him relay to Mr. Caspar that Charlie made it home and is now taking Lolly to the library. Thank you." She ended the call, grabbed Lolly's hand and left the house.

Less than twenty steps brought them to the front of the old colonial house that had been converted into the library. The wide front porch had several rocking chairs for patrons to use when they just wanted to sit outside and read a book.

Charlie and Lolly had spent a few beautiful summer days reading on that front porch. Now, they pushed through the front door with the open sign hanging in the window.

"Ms. Florence?" Charlie called out.

When she got no answer, she didn't worry. Rebecca sometimes was in the back kitchen making tea.

Charlie and Lolly laid their books on the return counter and went in search of some they hadn't read.

After a few minutes, Charlie went in search of Rebecca. She hoped the librarian could help her find more information on grazing rights and what it meant to the ranchers in the area.

She understood many of the ranchers had grazed their cattle on government land for years. Some families had been grazing cattle on government land for several generations. Paying a grazing fee wasn't the only expense they incurred. They were responsible for maintaining the fences on the land where they grazed their cattle and providing for the water, if it wasn't readily available.

"Rebecca?" Charlie pushed through a swinging door leading into the back of the house where the kitchen was. As soon as she passed through the door, she heard a soft moan, coming from the other side of an island.

Her heart slammed hard against her ribs and she ran forward.

Rebecca lay on the floor, her strawberry blond hair tangled and matted with blood. A gash on her forehead dripped blood into her eyes and onto the floor.

"Rebecca?" Charlie leaned down and grabbed the woman's hand. "What happened to you?"

"Charlie?" she said, though her voice sounded muffled. She tried to open her eyes, but couldn't seem to. Instead she gripped Charlie's hand. "Get out."

"What?" Charlie shook her head. "I'm not leaving until I get you some help."

"Go," she said. "Not safe." She coughed and spit up blood.

"Is the man who attacked you still here?"

She lay still for a moment before answering. "I don't think so." Her words ended on a moan.

Anger burned in Charlie's gut. How could anyone do this to as gentle a soul as Rebecca?

Charlie smoothed a lock of her reddish-blond hair from her face. "I'm calling the sheriff and an ambulance." She started to rise, but Rebecca tightened her hold on her hand.

"Angry. Said I told."

"Who was it?"

"Don't know." She coughed, her body tensing.

"Wore a mask. Said I...was ruining...everything..." Her grip loosened and her hand dropped to the floor.

Her throat constricting, Charlie pressed her fingers to the base of Rebecca's throat, hoping to find a pulse and nearly crying when she felt the reassuring thump against her fingertips. She stood and feverishly searched the kitchen for a telephone. Thankfully, there was one on the wall near the back door.

Charlie grabbed the phone and dialed 911. After passing the information to the dispatcher, she hung up and dialed Kevin's number.

Kevin answered the phone on the first ring. "Garner speaking."

"Kevin. Thank God. It's Charlie."

"What's wrong?"

"Rebecca Florence was attacked here in the library. I've notified 911. But she was more worried about me than herself. She said the guy who attacked her was angry. She said he was mad because she told. Is Ghost with you?"

"He just left to go to your house. He should be there about now."

Charlie dropped the phone as the sound of a siren wailed toward the little house. She pushed through the swinging door, suddenly afraid for her daughter she'd left in the children's section of the library.

"Lolly!" she shouted.

Lolly emerged from the front room, carrying

a colorful book, her brow pressed into a frown. "What's wrong?"

Charlie gathered her into her arms and hugged her close.

Ghost slammed through the front entrance, his eyes wide and his face tense until he spotted Charlie and Lolly. "Are you two okay?"

Charlie nodded and then tipped her head toward the kitchen door. "But Rebecca isn't. Could you take Lolly while I help her?"

"You stay with Lolly. I've had training in first aid." He stepped past her and entered the kitchen.

A few minutes later, a young sheriff's deputy entered the library, his gun drawn.

"I don't think you'll need that," Charlie said. They didn't need some rookie deputy shooting a man who was only attempting to render aid. "Jon Caspar is in the kitchen with Ms. Florence. He's one of the good guys."

The deputy didn't lower his weapon, instead, he entered the kitchen. Voices sounded through the wood paneling of the door.

Moments later the fire department paramedics entered. Charlie directed them to the kitchen and then pulled Lolly into the front parlor of the old house that Rebecca had designated as the children's room.

While she waited for Ghost to emerge from the kitchen, she read a story to Lolly.

"Mommy, you're not doing a very good job," Lolly said.

"Then *you* read it to *me*," she said, too tired to argue with her daughter.

Lolly read the story, slowing over some words, but far advanced for her age.

Charlie only half listened, her chest tight, her stomach knotted. When she saw the paramedic wheel Rebecca through the house on a stretcher, she stood.

Ghost followed, stopping in the doorway.

Charlie ran into his arms and hugged him around the middle. "Is she going to be all right?"

Ghost smoothed the hair on the back of her head. "I believe so. She took a pretty hard hit to the forehead. They'll keep her in the hospital to observe for concussion. Before she passed out, did she say who did it?"

"She didn't know. Apparently he wore a mask." Charlie wrung her hands. "I think she was attacked because of me." She stared up into Ghost's eyes, her own filling with tears. "I couldn't live with myself if something happened to her because of me."

"Why because of you?"

Her stomach roiled. "She said he attacked her because she told."

"Why would he attack *her*, if he was looking for *you*?"

"He might have thought she was me. I was tapped into the library Wi-Fi when I was looking at the social media site. I have auburn hair, Rebecca has strawberry blond. The picture he sent was not absolutely clear, he could have mistaken her for me."

"That's it. I'm staying with you and Lolly."

"Okay."

He went off as if she'd never spoken. "Until we know what's going on, you and I need to stick together. No argument."

Her lips twitched as she touched a hand to his chest. "I said okay."

Ghost stopped talking and stared down into her eyes. "About time we agreed on something." He bent to capture her lips in a soul-defining, earth-shattering kiss that left her boneless. She leaned against him, completely dependent on his strength to hold her up.

He glanced down at Lolly staring up at them. "Yes, Lolly, I kissed your mother."

GHOST KEPT IT together all the way back to Charlie's house. He couldn't tell her that hearing her crying out Lolly's name with a touch of panic in her voice had made his heart practically explode out of his chest. Then seeing what had happened to Rebecca and knowing it could have been Charlie made him nearly crumple to his knees.

He'd been back only a day and already he was as deeply in love with Charlie as he'd been seven years ago. The connection they'd shared had never quite gone away, instead it was there and stronger than before. The things he knew, the places he'd been and the experiences he'd survived made him even more aware of how fleeting life could be. One day a man could be on the earth, alive and healthy. The next, he could be six feet under or in the case of the two BLM men, they could have fallen into a toxic pit, leaving nothing left to identify.

He'd had friends die in his arms. He carried the pain with him every day of his life, never quite able to erase the images of them. They seemed to line up at night and dare him to sleep.

Knowing that could have been Charlie on the floor of the library left him feeling more panicked and uncertain than ever. He hadn't come back to find her, but fate placed her directly in his path and revealed to him the fact he had a child. How could he not stay and protect the two women who meant the most to him?

"You two stay here." Before he could allow them to go much farther than the front entryway, Ghost thoroughly searched the entire house. As soon as the guy who had attacked Rebecca discovered she wasn't the one he was after, he'd come back.

Ghost had to be ready.

When he returned, he found Charlie holding Lolly in her arms. The little girl was sobbing on her mother's shoulder.

Ghost's heart broke at the sound of the child's sobs. "Hey, what's all this?" he said softly.

"Ms. Florence is hurt." She sniffed and leaned back to look at Ghost. Her eyes were red-rimmed and puffy and tears stained her cheeks.

"Come here." He held out his arms. When Lolly went to him, his chest swelled two times bigger. She trusted him enough to come to him when she was distressed. That meant a lot.

Charlie stood with her hand on her daughter's back, her own eyes suspiciously glassy.

Holding Lolly in one arm, he opened the other.

Charlie stepped in and wrapped her arms around him and Lolly. For a long moment, the three of them remained in the tight hug.

Ghost had no desire to break it off anytime soon. The scent of Lolly's hair filled his nostrils. Baby shampoo and fresh air. He inhaled deeply and kissed the top of her head. Then he dropped a kiss on Charlie's temple, wishing he hadn't been such an idiot when he'd been there last. If he hadn't told her he wasn't interested in a long-term relationship, she might have let him in on the secret of his child. He wouldn't have missed all of her firsts. The first tooth, the first time she giggled. Her first step.

As he stood with his arms full of the two women he loved, he came to the conclusion he had to give up something. His career as a Navy SEAL or the family he'd just discovered.

He didn't want to give up either, but he had no right to ask Charlie and Lolly to wait around for him when he went out on missions. So many SEALs were divorced or never married. The waiting killed relationships. Most women wanted their man at home at night. Every night. And the worry of whether or not he'd come home alive, not in a body bag, was real and destructive to a spouse's peace of mind.

When his leg started aching and he couldn't stand still another minute longer, he asked, "Who wants hot cocoa?"

Lolly lifted her head from his shoulder. "Me."

"Me," Charlie agreed. "I'll fix it."

"No. Let me. Just point me in the right direction." He handed Lolly to her mother. "I can make a great cup of cocoa."

"We can all help." Charlie set Lolly on her feet and took her hand.

Lolly slipped her free hand in Ghost's and they entered the kitchen together. In a few short minutes, Ghost had the hot cocoa ready and Charlie made hot dogs for lunch.

"I know I bought ketchup," she said, sorting through the bottles of condiments in the refrigerator. When she didn't find it there, she went to the pantry. After a moment, she came back to the table with mustard. "I'm sorry. I must have forgotten it at the store."

"I put it in the refrigerator," Lolly said. She jumped up and went to the appliance and yanked open the door. "I put it right here." She pointed to an empty spot in the door.

"Well, it's not there," Charlie said. "You'll have to have mustard or eat your hot dog plain."

Lolly's bottom lip stuck out and she frowned. "I guess I'll eat mine plain." She sat at the table, and nibbled at the naked hot dog and drank the hot cocoa, gaining a white melted-marshmallow mustache on her upper lip.

Charlie slathered mustard on her hot dog and ate.

Ghost filled his bun with mustard and sweet relish and savored every bite. "That was delicious."

"Sweetheart," Charlie said softly to Lolly. "If you're done with your lunch, you can take your plate to the sink and go play in your room."

"Okay." She slid out of her chair and carried the plate to the sink.

As the child left the room, Charlie grimaced. "She usually won't eat a hot dog without the requisite ketchup."

Ghost smiled. "A girl who knows what she likes.

We'll have to ease her into mustard and relish. It's an acquired taste. But so good."

Charlie stared at him for a moment, her brows pinched lightly.

Ghost tried to think of what he'd said that would make her stare at him with that look of concern.

"Now that you know about Lolly, what are you going to do?"

He glanced in the direction Lolly had gone, not wanting to discuss the future of their daughter in front of her. "If you're finished with your meal, let's take this discussion out on the back porch."

He gathered her plate and his and carried them to the sink.

"Leave them. I'll take care of them later." She led the way to the back door and waited for him to follow before she opened it wide, stopped dead in her tracks and gasped.

Ghost nearly bumped into her, she stopped so fast.

There on the porch was the bottle of ketchup and written in bright red tomato sauce were the words *I KNOW WHERE YOU LIVE.*

Chapter Six

Charlie staggered backward into Ghost's arms. He pulled her away from the door and closed it between them and the damning writing on the porch.

"How did he get in?" Charlie turned and buried her face in Ghost's chest. "I'm positive I locked the doors."

"I double-checked the windows, as well as the doors." He smoothed his hand over the back of her head, his voice low and steady. "He must have picked the lock."

"He knows who I am, and he knows now where I live. He must have figured out Rebecca wasn't the one who tapped into his messages. We're not safe. I should pack up, take Lolly and leave."

"Then he wins."

"Good God, Ghost!" She slapped her palms on his chest. "This isn't a game."

"To him, it might be." He held her arms and stared

down into her face. "He might follow you wherever you go."

"Or not. He might be trying to scare me away from Grizzly Pass until he and his following do whatever dastardly deed they have planned." She shook her head and stared at the closest button on his shirt. "I can't risk Lolly's life on a game some psycho is playing with me."

"You forget something."

"What?" She stared up at him, her eyes a little wild, scared.

"You forget that you have me."

"I could have been in the library when he attacked Rebecca," she said, a shiver slithering down the back of her neck. "You weren't there."

"I will be from now on. And you can't go any-where without me until we catch the bastard."

"Then he wins by making me a prisoner in my own home." Charlie spun out of Ghost's grip and walked across the kitchen and back. "Look, you can stay until we figure this out. But you have to sleep on the couch. We're not picking up where we left off seven years ago. I'm a different person than the naive girl I was back then."

He nodded. "Agreed." He grinned. "About the couch and about being different. You're a much more beautiful woman, you're more independent and an incredible mother."

"And…" Her chin lifted and she captured his gaze with a cool steady one of her own. "I don't need anyone else in my life to make me happy," she insisted, if not to convince him, to convince herself.

"And you don't need anyone else in your life to make you happy," he repeated. "I get that. But when you're ready to talk, I want to discuss who Lolly needs in *her* life."

Charlie pinched the bridge of her nose and shook her head. "Can we postpone that one for another day? I have ketchup bleeding in my mind. And I'm not ready to start a custody battle."

He stepped toward her, his hand outstretched. "It doesn't have to be a battle."

She backed up. "No? I can't see anything but a battle in our future." When he opened his mouth, she held up both hands. "Please. For now, let's not go there. I can't deal with everything and a terrorist out to kill me." She looked at the floor, seeing Rebecca's limp body lying in her own blood. "I can't believe he attacked Rebecca. She wouldn't hurt a fly." She glanced up. "And it's my fault. If I hadn't been snooping on the internet for a few measly dollars extra, none of this would have happened."

"Darlin', you can't blame yourself. You didn't hurt Rebecca. *He* did. We'll deal with this together."

Though her heart warmed when he referred to her as darlin', she couldn't ignore the most important part of the equation. "What about Lolly? I don't want her to be collateral damage. She's just a child." God, what had she done? This was supposed to be an easy gig. She was supposed to be anonymous. No one would know she was the one surfing, searching for terrorist activities.

"Tell you what," Ghost said. "I'll have Garner bring new locks and keys. I can install them today."

She shook her head. "What good will that do? He'll just pick those, too."

Ghost shrugged. "It'll make *me* feel better."

She flipped her hand. "Fine. And I can get online and see if I can find the IP address of the social media group. Maybe we can chase down the leader through it."

"Garner will have Hack working on that, as well."

She nodded. "I did give him the URL. I would think Hack could find it before I can, but two heads are better than one."

Ghost clapped his hands together. "Good. You have a plan. I have a plan. Let's get to it."

Charlie went back to work in her office, searching through the internet, looking for the IP address that the Free America group occupied.

She could hear Ghost placing a call to Kevin, explaining what had happened with the ketchup. Half an hour later, a man she didn't know arrived at her door.

Apparently, Ghost did, calling him by an unusual nickname. "Hey, Caveman. Thanks for bringing these."

"I'm staying to help install them," Caveman said.

"That'll get it done faster," Ghost agreed. "Thanks."

They didn't ask her opinion or assistance, which was perfectly okay with her. Charlie didn't leave her office, except to check on Lolly. She spent the afternoon trying everything she knew, and searching the internet for techniques she didn't know that could help her find the man who'd threatened her online.

About the time Caveman left, Charlie could hear the two men talking softly near the front door, their voices carrying down the hallway, but not clearly enough to make out their words.

Charlie didn't care. She trusted Ghost to keep her and Lolly safe. She had to get to the bottom of who was threatening her, or she'd have no peace.

Ghost appeared in the doorway a few minutes later, carrying a cup of hot tea. "Any luck?"

"I wish I could say yes, but I'm no computer forensics expert. That's not what I studied in my Information Systems degree."

"So you've been in school again?"

She nodded.

"You had just completed a degree when we met seven years ago."

"In business. It was pretty general. When I realized I was pregnant, I knew I had to get something with more of a skill I could work with at home. So I went into Information Systems and learned about databases, data management, design and programming."

"I'm impressed."

She shrugged. "My goal was to work from home so that I could live wherever I wanted." And she'd wanted to come home to Grizzly Pass to raise Lolly. It was a more laid-back and safe environment. Until now.

"I'm impressed. You've been busy."

"What about you?" She'd been dying to ask, but hadn't wanted to know more about him that would make her fall more deeply in love with the man. Still she couldn't resist knowing what he'd gone through in the past seven years. "Are you still based out of California?"

"I'm out of Virginia, now. I completed some training in riverine ops with SEAL Boat Team 22 out of Stennis Space Center in Mississippi. I've had over forty deployments since last we saw each other. But I've also managed to complete my online degree in financial management. Since I'm rarely in town, I don't have time to spend the money I make. I invest it."

She smiled up at him. "You've been busy, too."

He nodded. "Anything I can do to help?"

Her lips twisted and she shook her head. "Not unless you're an experienced hacker, along with being a trained SEAL."

He disappeared, leaving her to her work.

Charlie's senses were tuned into his movements. She could tell when he'd gone into Lolly's bedroom. Their voices drifted to her, making her want to give up on her search and join them. Normally, she would break from her work for the Bozeman software company to spend time with her daughter. But what she was doing was more important. She couldn't let the man threatening her get away with it. And since he'd attacked Rebecca, apparently he would follow through on his threat.

Charlie shivered and dug deeper, following leads on the computer, searching through videos on how to find an IP address. Everything she tried ran her into a brick wall.

The smell of cooking onions drifted into her office and brought her out of her focused concentration.

Ghost was in the kitchen and, by the sound of it, Lolly was helping. Charlie smiled. At least her daughter had a chance to get to know the man who was her father.

Ghost was a good man. Charlie shouldn't have kept the news of his daughter from him. He'd missed so much of her life already and it wouldn't be fair of her to keep him from seeing her in the future. They'd have to come up with a plan to trade off on weekends and holidays.

The thought saddened her. Charlie had grown up with parents who had been married for more than thirty years. They were still as in love with each other as the day they'd met. Their marriage was the standard by which Charlie measured all other relationships.

Perhaps theirs was the exception, not the rule. Wasn't having a part-time father who loved her better than no father at all? She had a lot of thinking to do, and perhaps this wasn't the time to do it. Her problems were more immediate than setting up a visitation schedule.

Lolly appeared in the doorway with a hand-folded paper hat on her head and a towel over her shoulder. She stood straight, her lips twitching. "Your dinner is served," she said in her most formal tone. She spoiled the effect by giggling. "Come on, Mommy. Mr. Caspar and I set the table. We made a lasagna for dinner."

"Lasagna?" Charlie's stomach rumbled. "It smells wonderful."

"It is wonderful." The child grabbed her hand and pulled Charlie to her feet. "Hurry. I'm hungry."

Charlie chuckled and let her daughter practically drag her down the hallway to the kitchen.

Ghost stood at the sink, an apron looped around his neck and tied around his narrow waist. He glanced over his shoulders. "Have a seat. Dinner is just about done."

"Can I do anything?" Charlie asked.

"You can sit down and look beautiful with Lolly." He winked at the little girl. "She even brushed her own hair and changed into that dress."

Lolly nodded. "All by myself."

Charlie stood back, studying her daughter's clothes and hair. "Good job." She gave her a high five and pulled out a chair for her daughter to slide into.

Dinner was perfect. The lasagna tasted so good, Charlie accepted a second helping and ate until she was so full, she couldn't form a coherent thought. "What did you put into that pasta? I suspect it was some kind of sleeping potion." A yawn slipped out and she covered her mouth. "I think I'll get a shower and go to bed." She glanced at Lolly. "Are you about done?"

"Don't worry about Lolly. She and I have a date with her favorite book tonight. I'll help her through bath time and pajamas. Go. Get your shower and sleep."

Charlie didn't argue. The stress of the day and

not being able to sleep the night before had left her exhausted. She trudged her way to the bathroom, stripped down and stepped beneath the spray. If she wasn't so tired, she'd be tempted to invite Ghost to join her.

Her eyes widened. What was she thinking? Invite Ghost in the shower with her? She wasn't a twenty-two-year-old anymore. Ghost wasn't going to be around forever, and she refused to put herself and Lolly through the heartbreak of a man entering and leaving her life with no commitment to return.

He might be okay with that lifestyle, but she couldn't take that yo-yo effect. Lord forbid if he should bring back a wife on one of his visits to Lolly.

Her hands clenched and heat burned through her body. She twisted the knob on the faucet to cold and stood beneath the showerhead, letting the water chill her until she shivered.

Then she remembered she hadn't grabbed a towel from the hall linen closet. She stepped out of the shower onto the bath mat, dripping wet and chilled to the bone. Grabbing her shirt, she held it up to her chest and opened the door a crack. No one was in the hallway. She could hear voices in the kitchen. With the coast clear, she darted across the hall to the closet, flung open the door and snatched a towel. She had just turned to dash back into the bathroom when the wood floor squeaked at the other end of the hallway and she heard Ghost say, "I'm going to check to see if your mother is finished in the shower. I'll be right back."

She didn't make it across the hall. Her feet froze to the floor. Holding the towel in front of her, she couldn't think, couldn't move and only stared at Ghost.

His gaze slipped over her, traveling slowly downward from her face to her breasts, where she'd pressed the towel to the swells. Lower still, his gaze moved to the flare of her hips, clearly visible with the towel draped down only the middle of her torso.

His eyes flared and his body stiffened.

Heat rose from Charlie's core and spread throughout her body. The moisture from that short, cold shower steamed off her body as passion flared and burned a path outward, making her ache for him in every part of her existence.

"Charlie." The word came out in a low, sexy tone. He stepped toward her, his hand reaching out.

Charlie was caught in the spell, the temptation to run into his arms so strong, her arm relaxed, the towel inching downward.

"Mr. Caspar?" Lolly called out from the kitchen.

And snap. Just like that, the spell was broken.

Charlie flung herself into the bathroom, closed

the door and leaned her back against it, breathing hard as if she'd run a marathon instead of three feet across the hallway.

From sleepy to wide-awake in two seconds flat. She scrubbed her body with the towel, hoping the added abrasion would push Ghost out of her mind. It had the opposite effect. Her skin tingled from the heated gaze he'd spread over her body. Her nipples were tight, puckered for his touch.

She moaned, threw the towel onto the floor and stomped it. "No. No. No. I will not make love to that man."

"Everything all right in there?" Ghost's voice sounded through the door. Was that a chuckle she heard?

Charlie channeled her desire into something just as heated. Anger. Shoving her head into her night-gown, she pulled it down over her body and slipped her arms into the matching robe. Then she frowned, fearing the garment was a little too revealing. Since she didn't have anything else with her in the bath-room, she sighed. It would have to do. She reached for her panties, but the counter was bare.

Damn. Had she forgotten them? She opened the door and peered out.

Ghost stood in the hallway, dangling a pair

of soft blue bikini panties from his index finger. "Missing something?"

Her eyes widened and she reached for the panties.

He pulled them back at the last minute.

Charlie's forward momentum carried her toward him and she slammed into his chest.

Ghost clamped an arm around her waist and held her tight against him. "You felt it, too, didn't you?"

"I don't know what you're talking about." She reached for the panties again, her breasts rubbing against his chest through the thin fabric of her nightgown. "Let me have those."

He raised his eyebrows. "Say *please*."

She gritted her teeth, her core tightening, the ache building the longer she stood with her nearly naked body pressed to his. Instead of arguing over underwear, she wanted to wrap her legs around his waist. Hell, she wanted him inside her, filling that space that had been empty for so long. God, she'd missed him. And she'd miss him when he was gone.

Charlie slumped in his arms. "Fine. You can keep them. But let me go. There really can't be anything between us."

His arm tightened around her. "Why?"

"You have your responsibilities. I have mine. I gave you my heart once. I'm not willing to do it again."

For a long moment, he held her in his arms, his gaze locked on hers.

She refused to look away first. Losing him the first time had been so hard. Carrying his baby, knowing he wouldn't be a part of their lives had nearly killed her. She couldn't let him back into her life, only to have him leave again and break not only her heart, but Lolly's, too.

FINALLY, GHOST LOOSENED his hold. He could see the hurt in Charlie's eyes and he wanted to take it all away. He'd caused that. He'd been the one to break her heart. If he wanted her back, he'd have to earn her trust.

He released her, but he didn't hand back her panties. Instead, he wadded them up and shoved them into his pocket. Yeah, it might be juvenile, but he wanted something that belonged to her, should she end up kicking him out of her life. "Lolly's ready for her bath and bedtime story."

"I can take care of her."

"Get her through her bath. I'll take it from there."

"You don't need to. I'm awake now."

"I don't care if you're awake. I want to read to my daughter—to get to know her." His mouth formed a thin line, his brows dipping low. "At least give me that."

She nodded. "Fair enough." Charlie stepped away from him, spun on her heels and walked into her bedroom.

Knowing she wasn't wearing panties nearly made Ghost come undone. The sway of her hips and the way she flung her damp hair over her shoulder was so enticing, he almost went after her. The way her nipples puckered, making little tents in her silky nightgown, was proof she wasn't immune to him.

Yeah, he had a long way to go to convince her he was worth a second chance.

You broke my heart once...

Was he selfish to want her back? He adjusted his jeans to accommodate his natural reaction to her bare-bottom state. Hell, yeah, it was selfish. What he needed to consider was if he was the man for her. Charlie was special. She deserved someone who could be there for her always.

As a Navy SEAL, he couldn't be in Wyoming except when he took leave. If she and Lolly wanted to be with him, they'd have to leave Wyoming and join him at Little Creek, Virginia. Even then, they'd only see him when he wasn't deployed. The advantage to living on or near a Navy base was the support network of the military and other military spouses.

God, she deserved so much more.

After his last deployment and being injured, Ghost had worried he wouldn't get the medical clearance to return to his unit. Now he wondered if it wasn't time for him to step down. Take a medical retirement, find a less dangerous job that allowed him to be home more often.

He walked back into the kitchen to find Lolly drying the last plate.

"I couldn't reach the cabinet." She pointed upward.

Ghost opened the cabinet and set the cleaned and dried plates inside. Then he dropped his hand to the top of Lolly's soft, red hair. He wanted the chance to be with his daughter. To get to know her, and for her to get to know him. Dragging them around the nation was selfish. But, damn it. He wanted to be a part of Lolly's life, even if Charlie didn't want anything else to do with him.

"Come on, it's time for your bath and a bedtime story." He held out his hand.

Lolly laid hers in his, so trusting. Would she be better off with a stepdad who could be there for her? Would he be kind to her and treat her like she was his own daughter?

Ghost couldn't imagine Lolly with any other father, any more than he could imagine Charlie with another man.

"You get your pjs while I run the water."

"Roger," she said and grinned up at him. "I said that right, didn't I?"

He'd been teaching her how SEALs talked to each other. The child picked up quickly. Smart as a whip. Just like her mother.

"Roger." He gave her a nudge toward her bedroom. "Go. Get those pjs." Ghost entered the bathroom. It still smelled like Charlie's shampoo, making him want to skip Lolly's bath and go straight into her mother's bedroom, climb into her bed and make crazy, passionate love to her.

Instead, he sat on the side of the bathtub, turned the handles on the faucet and adjusted the temperature to just right for a six-year-old.

Lolly entered carrying her colorful pjs, tossed them on the counter and stuck her hand in the water. "Just right."

"Need any help here? If not, I'll go find the perfect book for us to read together."

"I can take my own bath. Mommy thinks I need help, but I don't." She puffed out her chest and lifted her chin, just like Charlie did when she was standing up for herself or someone else. Lolly was so much like her mother, it made Ghost's chest hurt just looking at her.

"Okay, then." He dropped a kiss on top of her head and left her to do her thing, propping the bathroom door open so he could listen for her.

He walked back to the living room, found the phone and dialed the number for Garner.

"Charlie, how's it going?"

"It's Ghost," he said. "So far we're okay. What's the status on the librarian?"

"She's holding her own. Minor swelling on the brain. They're watching her closely and keeping her sedated. By all indications, she'll live."

"I also wanted to know if Hack found anything in those messages that would lead us to whoever has targeted Charlie."

"Nothing so far. He's close to finding the IP address. As soon as he does, I'll send one of the guys out to recon."

"I'd like to be the one to corner that man."

"You and me both. He's a slick bastard. But I find it hard to believe a rancher or pipeliner is crafty enough to pull off a takeover without some help from outside."

Ghost's fists clenched. "You think the ranchers and pipeliners are too dumb to pull this off?"

"No, no. Don't get me wrong. I think they're plenty smart. I just don't know that they could pull it off without some tactical training and influence from outside the ranching and pipeline community."

"So far, all I've seen in the way of an uprising was the ranchers protesting the confiscation of a herd of cattle. Was anyone arrested?"

"No. As long as there was no harm to anyone and no property damage, they were free to protest."

"Did you or one of the others get some names of the primary instigators?"

"Hawkeye spoke with one rancher who had twenty-eight hundred head of cattle confiscated, LeRoy Vanders," Garner said. "He was hopping mad and ready to rip into the BLM."

"And?"

"The sheriff managed to calm him. The crowd has since dissipated, but there are a lot of angry ranchers. Hack's checking online records for some of the names Hawkeye came up with from the protesters. T-Rex will be positioning himself at the County Line Bar tonight to make some new friends among the survivalist groups."

"What about Hawkeye?"

"He'll be downstairs in the Tavern striking up conversations with the ranchers and unemployed pipeline workers who come in each night to get a drink and commiserate."

"Mr. Caspar?" Lolly called out from down the hall.

Ghost lowered his voice. "I have to go. Let us know anything you might find out about the man stalking Ms. McClain. As *soon* as you find out. Even if it's in the middle of the night."

"Roger," Garner said. "I'll have Caveman swing by a couple of times during the night."

"Thanks," Ghost said. "Out here." He ended the call and hurried down the hall to the bathroom.

Lolly was out of the tub, wearing her panties,

her nightgown pulled over her head, but stuck half-way down.

Ghost untangled the gown and dragged the hem downward to her knees.

She smiled up at him. "Thank you." Then she skipped past him to her bedroom and selected a book from her shelf. "Read this," she demanded.

Ghost took the book from her. "Did you brush your teeth?"

She clapped a hand to her mouth and darted for the door. "I'll be right back."

He grinned and waited for her, thumbing through the book she'd chosen about a little girl pretending to be a beauty shop lady. He chuckled at some of the descriptions. Then he turned down the comforter on Lolly's bed and sat on the edge.

Lolly was back in two minutes, smiling wide. "Clean. See?"

He frowned down at her. "You sure you brushed long enough?"

She nodded. "I sang 'Happy Birthday' all the way through twice."

"Okay. Let's find out what's going on in this book." Ghost opened the book and started reading, getting as caught up in the character's plight as Lolly by the end of the story.

"Now, this one," Lolly insisted, opening another book and handing it to him.

After reading two more books, Ghost told Lolly it was time to close her eyes and go to sleep.

Lolly pouted for a brief moment and then flopped down on her back and burrowed into the sheets and comforter, until all Ghost could make out was Lolly's cute little head poking out of the big bed. "Aren't you going to stay?" She patted the bed beside her.

Ghost sat on the edge of the bed and bent to kiss her good-night. She captured his head between her palms and kissed him soundly on the cheek.

He laughed and kissed the top of her head. "Good night, princess."

"Good night, Mr. Caspar." She yawned, stretched and closed her eyes. "I love you."

Ghost's heart squeezed hard in his chest. Those three little words practically brought him to his knees. The child hardly knew him, but she trusted him to take care of her and to be there when she woke up.

He wanted to gather her in his arms and hold her tight. Forever. His little girl.

In less than five minutes she was asleep, her breathing slow and steady. But Ghost remained perched on the side of her bed, watching her angelic face as she slept, and his heart grew fuller by the minute.

If anyone tried to hurt her... His fists clenched. He'd rip the attacker apart, one limb at a time. No one messed with his family.

"No one," he whispered.

Chapter Seven

Charlie woke with a start and stared into the darkness. She'd had a dream about someone chasing her through the rooms of the library next door. He'd almost captured her, when she'd forced herself to wake.

Her heart thundered against her ribs and perspiration beaded on her forehead. A glance at the clock indicated she'd been asleep for four hours. She hadn't even heard when Lolly went to bed. That was a first in the six years she'd been a mother. Going to sleep before her daughter wasn't something she ever did. It was a testament to the trust she had in Ghost.

Which reminded her. Though she trusted him to keep her and her daughter safe through the night, she shouldn't trust him with her heart. She wasn't sure she would survive a second time around of a broken heart.

Shoving aside the covers she got out of bed and padded barefoot down the hallway to Lolly's bedroom.

Her daughter lay curled on her side, an arm wrapped around her favorite teddy bear and sleeping peacefully with a smile curling her lips. A few books lay on the nightstand beside her bed.

Charlie smiled, imagining Ghost reading them to her daughter. She'd have him reading more than that if he let her talk him into it.

Tucking the blanket around Lolly's chin, she bent to kiss her daughter's cheek.

Lolly rolled over and whispered, "I love you, Mr. Caspar."

Charlie's breath caught at the constriction in her throat. Her daughter was already falling in love with the man who'd broken Charlie's heart seven years ago. Would Lolly's little heart be broken as well when Ghost left to return to his SEAL team?

On silent feet, she tiptoed down the hallway where she peered into the living room.

Ghost lay in the lounge chair, shirtless, wearing boxer shorts and nothing else. He leaned back, his arms crossed over his chest, his eyes closed and his breathing deep and regular. Asleep.

Charlie took the opportunity to drink her fill of him, studying his face, chest, arms and thick, muscular thighs. How she wished she could go to him, straddle his waist and press her hot center to him. She had yet to find another pair of panties. She wondered what he'd done with the ones he'd taken.

That he wanted to keep them must mean something. But what? That he wanted to make love to her? She had no doubt about that. When he'd held her close, the ridge beneath his jeans had been firm and insistent, pressing against her belly.

Warmth spread through her body, igniting the flames at her center. She burned uncontrollably, wanting the man more than she'd wanted anyone or anything in her life. If she gave in to her carnal lust, he wouldn't resist. Hell, he'd welcome her with the same level of passion. Their sex life had never been the problem between them.

Yeah, Charlie had told Ghost she didn't care if a relationship with him was only temporary. But that had been before she'd discovered she was in love with him. When he'd left, she'd held it together until that night when she'd been alone in her bed. Then she'd cried. And cried some more. Two weeks later, she was crying even harder when she discovered she'd missed her period and the early pregnancy test proved positive.

Seven years ago, she'd given her heart to this man. And based on the way she felt at that moment, she still loved him. If not as much, then even more.

Her eyes stinging, Charlie backed away from

the living room and escaped into the kitchen. She peered through the curtain over the window on the back door. Moonlight shone onto the porch, bathing everything in a dark blue glow.

The ketchup had been cleaned off the wooden planks. She'd have to thank Ghost in the morning. It was one fewer thing she had to face on her own. Though the message was gone, it remained seared into her mind.

Unable to face going back to her lonely bed, Charlie tiptoed into her office, half closing the door. She booted her computer and went to work, trying to find the man responsible for the attack on Rebecca and the ketchup message on her back porch. The threats had to stop. Both to herself and to whatever government facility he had in mind by his call to arms.

She returned to the site with the entries from people who had legitimate gripes with the way they'd been treated by local and national authorities. One by one, she followed each posting, tracking them back to their own social media pages. Each had pictures of their families posted. These were real people with loved ones. All they wanted was to be treated fairly. They were all upset about the confiscation of LeRoy Vanders's herd, wanting the authorities to return the man's animals as they were his livelihood. If he couldn't get them back, he wouldn't have the means to provide for his family. He'd posted, You might as well shoot me now. I'm worth more to my family dead than alive.

She followed LeRoy to his page. There he had posted messages from Bible scripture, praying for a peaceful resolution to the current crisis. It didn't sound like a man crazy enough to threaten someone for spying on his messages.

But then Charlie didn't know what set a man like that off. If desperate enough, he might go off the deep end and come out fighting.

She tried scanning the internet for other terrorist threats that could be tied to the state of Wyoming. At one point she found a message from a man claiming to be a member of ISIS. His threat was to all American infidels. He was coming. Be prepared to convert or die.

A shiver rippled across her as she stared into the eyes of a man who looked like he could kill without it impacting him in the least. His brown eyes had that intense crazy look that burned into her, even from a computer screen.

Charlie pushed her chair away from the monitor and keyboard. She stood, stretched and walked to the window overlooking the street in front of her house. Moonlight streamed through the window, bathing her in its pale, blue glow.

Why did something so beautiful three nights ago seem so sinister now? She'd always loved nighttime in Wyoming. She'd loved staring up at the stars with her father, identifying constellations and planets.

The night she'd spent in the back of Ghost's pickup, they'd had fun naming different stars as if they were the scientists who'd discovered them. They laughed and rolled into each other's arms. A kiss led to a caress. The caress moved from outside their clothes to bare skin. Soon, they were naked, bathed in starlight, making love.

Charlie wrapped her arms around her middle and sighed. Why couldn't things have remained the same? That had been their last night together. The next day, he'd driven to his new assignment in California and she'd stayed in Wyoming, nursing a broken heart.

She raised her hand to push her hair back from her forehead.

Seven years later, he was in her living room, wearing nothing but boxer shorts, sexier than ever, and she was staring out at the night sky wishing for something that would only bring her more heartache.

"Hey." Ghost's voice echoed in her head, like a memory she couldn't forget. Why had she never been able to forget him? Why couldn't she ignore him now?

"Charlie, darlin'." That voice again, made the ache in her belly grow.

Big hands descended on her arms, turning her to face the man she'd never stopped loving.

GHOST HAD REMAINED in the doorway to Charlie's office for a long time before he'd made a sound.

She'd stood by the window, her body swathed in a pale glow turning her into an ethereal blue image of lush, unaffected beauty.

She was sexy, but appeared sad, staring out into the darkness. He wanted to tell her to step away from the window in case someone decided to take a shot at her. As still as she was, she'd make an easy target.

When she raised her arm to push her hair back the moonlight shone through the thin fabric of her nightgown, exposing the silhouette of her naked body beneath.

His breath lodged in his lungs, or he would have moaned aloud. Every cell in his body burned for her. His pulse sped through his veins carrying red-hot blood angling south to his groin. He had to have her, to hold her in his arms. To feel her skin against his.

"Hey," he managed to say.

When she didn't turn to face him, he eased into the room. Perhaps she'd been sleepwalking and wasn't hearing him through her dream.

"Charlie, darlin'," he whispered. Gripping her arms, he turned her toward him.

She glanced up at him, recognition in her gaze and something else. Longing. Pure, unrestricted passion.

Charlie pressed her hands to his chest and slid them up to lock around the back of his neck. Then she stood on her toes, pulling his head down to hers. "Call me all kinds of a fool, for making the same mistake twice, but I want you."

"If wanting you is a mistake, I don't care what you call me. Just let me have you for a moment," he said, drawing her into his arms. He wrapped his hands around her waist and pressed her hips against his. His erection swelled, pressing into her belly, when he'd rather be pressing it into her.

He claimed her mouth in a long, hard kiss. When he traced the seam of her lips, she opened to him, meeting his tongue with hers in a twisting tangle of urgency.

She drew her arms down his chest and around to his backside, sliding her fingers beneath the elastic of his boxers. Slim, warm hands cupped his buttocks and squeezed gently.

He broke the kiss, dragging in a deep breath, barely able to hold back, when wave after wave of lust washed over him, urging him to take her now. In the office, on the desk, against the wall. Anywhere he could get inside her. Now.

He bunched her nightgown in his hands, pulling it up over her bottom and groaned.

She hadn't found another pair of panties. Her sex was bared to him, there for the taking.

Ghost slid his hands down the backs of her thighs and lifted her, wrapping her legs around his waist.

She locked her ankles behind him and captured his face between her palms. "This is for now. Nothing has changed between us. Don't expect anything from me tomorrow."

His heart tightened in his chest. He understood why she said these things. She didn't trust him. Didn't expect him to stay and she had to guard her heart and Lolly's from the hurt she expected him to inflict when he left.

He knew all of this as the truth, but he couldn't stop. He had to have her. He'd work on the trust later. When he wasn't consumed by his need to feel her against him. The need to lose himself inside her.

He carried her down the hallway to her bedroom, careful not to make enough noise that would wake the little one. Once inside, he pushed the door half-closed with his foot and carried Charlie to the bed. "Protection?"

"I'm on birth control and I'm clean."

"I'm clean, too."

She kissed his lips and whispered against his mouth, "Then what are you waiting for?"

He sat her on the edge of the bed, grabbed the

hem of her nightgown and pulled it slowly over her head.

She raised her arms to accommodate the removal of her only garment. Charlie leaned back on her elbow in the glow of a night-light and spread her knees wide. She ran one hand down her belly to the triangle of curls covering her sex and threaded her fingers through them. She tipped her head toward his boxers. "Are you going to wear those all night?"

"Oh, hell no." Ghost shucked the shorts and stood before her, his shaft jutting out, his body on fire for her. His first inclination was to take her, hard and fast, to thrust deep inside her glistening entrance. But he didn't want to scare her away. He wanted her to know the depth of need and passion he was experiencing. Hell, he wanted to bring her to the very edge and make her beg for him to take her.

Ghost dropped to his knees in front of her and draped her legs over his shoulders.

Her eyes widened and her breathing became more labored. She threaded her fingers through the fluff of hair over her sex to the folds beneath.

Ghost stroked her hand and her fingers and brushed them aside to take over. He parted her folds, exposing the narrow strip of flesh between. Leaning in, he flicked her with the tip of his tongue.

She moved her hands, weaving them into his hair,

while digging her heels into his back, urging him to continue.

He tongued her again, this time swirling around, laving until she pulled on his hair, a moan rising from her throat.

Ghost remembered how she had given herself to him so completely when they were younger, yelling out his name in the throes of their shared passion. He wanted to capture that same sense of abandon.

While his tongue took control of her nubbin, he thrust one of his fingers into her slick channel, reveling in how wet she already was, knowing it would ease him inside her soon. He added a second finger in with the first and stretched her, feeling her muscles contract, gripping his fingers.

Teasing and tasting, he licked, swirled and flicked that amazing bundle of nerves that made her crazy with desire.

And she responded by raising her hips, pumping them upward, pulling on his hair to keep him focused on her pleasure.

He didn't need the encouragement. Making her come apart was his goal. If he read her right, she was nearing her climax.

Charlie's body tensed, her heels dug into his back and she thrust her hips upward.

Ghost didn't relent, continuing his frenzied assault until he stormed past her resistance.

Charlie's fingers curled into his scalp and she cried out softly, "Ghost!" as she gave in with abandon, her body shaking with her release.

Ghost continued to stroke her with his fingers and tongue, slowing the movement as she relaxed and sank back to the mattress.

"Oh, my," she said, her head tossing from side to side. "I didn't know it could be even better than before."

Ghost chuckled and scooted her up farther on the bed. He lay beside her, his hand cupping her sex, his shaft throbbing with his need. He wanted her to be sure.

She finally looked into his eyes, her own narrowing. "Why did you stop?"

"I want you to be sure."

"Sweet heaven. I've never been more sure." She dragged him over her, parted her legs and let him slide between them. "Please. Don't make me wait another minute."

Releasing a long breath, he eased up to her entrance, dipping in slowly. "Tell me to stop and I will."

"Don't you dare." She raised her legs, clamped them around his waist and dug her heels into his buttocks, urging him to take her. "I want you. All of you. Inside me. Now."

Unable to hold back another second, he drove into

her, thrusting all the way until he was completely encased in her slick, tight wetness.

He bent to kiss her, taking her tongue with his as he moved out and back into her. Slowly at first, then faster and faster until he pumped in and out of her like a piston in an engine.

The faster he went, the harder he got, the tension building, pushing him to the edge. One. Last. Thrust. And he shot into the stratosphere, spiraling to the stars, his body exploding with electric shocks that spread through him from his shaft to the very tips of his fingers. He dropped down on her, still buried deep inside and held steady until his shaft stopped throbbing and he could breathe normally again.

At long last, he rolled to his side and pulled her with him, curling her up against his body.

Charlie laid her cheek against his chest and chuckled. "Your heart is racing."

"You do that to me."

She sighed and circled her fingers around his hard, brown nipple. "I'd say I could get used to this, but I can't."

"Can't, or won't?"

"Does it matter?" she whispered. "You're here today. But you'll be gone soon."

"What if I come back?"

"In another seven years?" She snorted and shook her head.

"How about in a couple of months?"

"Would it be fair to Lolly?"

He thought about it. "I want to know my daughter. I want to watch her grow."

"You can't do that if you aren't here."

He knew what she said was true. But lots of SEALs had families willing to be there when they got home.

"Charlie, I want you—"

She pressed a finger to his lips. "Shh. I just want to hold you for tonight. We don't have to talk. In fact, I'd rather not ruin what we shared with words we might regret."

Ghost clamped his teeth down on his tongue, wanting to say more, wanting to force her into some kind of commitment, but he didn't want her to kick him out of her bed. For that night, he would shut up and hold her. Tomorrow, they'd have to make time to talk. They had too much at stake to remain silent for long.

Chapter Eight

Charlie lay in the warmth of Ghost's arms, listening to the beat of his heart. This was where she'd always wanted to be. She didn't want the night to end. For a long time, she lay awake, until her eyes closed and she drifted into sleep.

A sharp ringing sound jerked her out of a lovely dream, jarring her awake. She sat up, thinking it was the smoke alarm. When it stopped and then rang again, she realized it was the phone on the other side of the bed.

Ghost grabbed the phone from the cradle and handed it to her.

She took it, almost afraid to answer. "Hello," Charlie said, her voice hoarse with sleep.

"Ms. McClain, Hack here. You wanted me to call when we got a hit on the IP address."

Charlie sat up straighter, pushing the fog of sleep out of her head. "Whose is it?"

"We traced it back to a man who died several months ago, but I have one of our guys headed out to the physical address. Apparently it's local. I thought you'd want to know."

"I do. Is that all?"

"So far. I'm still tracking some of the people in that chat room. When I have more, I'll let you know."

"Thank you." She handed the phone to Ghost and he set it back on the charger.

"They're sending someone out to the physical address associated with the IP address," she said, draping her arm over her eyes.

Ghost rose up on his elbow and stared down at her. "Whose was it?"

She moved her arm and stared up into his eyes, her own narrowing. "That's the strange part. Hack said it was registered to a dead man."

"A what?" He brushed a strand of her hair from her face, tucking it behind her ear.

She leaned into his hand and kissed his palm. "Someone who'd died several months ago."

Ghost bent to kiss her forehead. "I would like to know if he died of natural causes, or if he was murdered." Then he kissed her nose.

Charlie closed her eyes, loving the feel of his lips on her skin, while blocking the thought of someone who might have been murdered for his connection to an IP address. She opened her eyes. "What time is it?"

Ghost leaned back to glance at the clock on the nightstand. "Nearly seven o'clock."

Her heart leaped. "Lolly will be up any minute." She shoved against his chest. "You have to get out of here."

"Why?"

"She's super curious and asks a lot of questions. Frankly, I'm not prepared to answer any about you."

"Like, 'Mommy, why are you in bed with Mr. Caspar? And why are you naked?'" He lowered the sheet and tweaked the tip of her nipple.

Her core responded with an answering ache. But she couldn't allow herself to go for round two with the chance of Lolly running in and jumping into the bed, like she did so often. As much as she would have liked to see his tweak and raise it to a much more satisfying conclusion, she didn't feel like facing a lot of questions from her daughter.

"Out." She rolled away and shot out of the bed.

Ghost got up and stretched, his body naked in the light peeking around the edges of the curtains. God, he was gorgeous.

A sound from the room down the hallway made her race to her closet, grab the first pair of jeans she could find and jam her legs into them. "For the love of Mike, cover yourself," she hissed. "Lolly's awake."

Ghost grabbed his boxers from the floor and slipped them up his thighs.

Charlie pulled a sweatshirt over her head and ran for the door. "I'll distract her while you find more clothes."

His laughter followed her out the door and down the hallway to Lolly's room.

Her chest swelled with an unbidden joy at the sound. The joy faded when she thought about the end of the week and his ultimate departure. She wasn't certain her heart could take the pain again. Refusing to think that far ahead, she entered Lolly's room and found her standing by the bed, pushing her bright auburn hair out of her face. "I'm hungry," she said.

"Let's get you dressed and then you can help me fix breakfast." Charlie spun her daughter away from the door and walked her over to her dresser.

As Charlie helped Lolly choose an outfit, out of the corner of her eye, she saw Ghost pass by in the hallway, with a big grin and a little wave.

When Lolly was dressed in a hot pink shirt, jeans and her pink cowboy boots, she was hard to hold back.

Charlie stepped out of her way, hoping Ghost was completely dressed and presentable. Apparently he was, because she heard Lolly in the kitchen talking to him.

With a few minutes to herself, Charlie washed

her face, brushed her hair and her teeth and dressed in something more attractive than jeans and a bulky sweatshirt. Feeling a little more put together in dark jeans, a white blouse and her cowboy boots, her curly hair secured behind her head in a barrette, she entered the kitchen to find Ghost and Lolly waiting for her, the stove cold, the kitchen table empty.

"We're going to have breakfast at the tavern," Lolly said, grinning.

"We are?" Charlie's gaze met Ghost's, her brows rising.

"We are. My treat," he said. "Shall we go?" He took Lolly's hand in his and cupped Charlie's elbow.

"Actually, it sounds good." She hadn't treated herself or Lolly to a breakfast out in a very long time. Eating at a fast-food restaurant in Bozeman on her way to drop Lolly at the daycare didn't count.

Ghost insisted on taking his truck, moving Lolly's booster seat into the back center seat of the crew cab. Lolly liked being high above the ground, claiming she could see everything.

Charlie climbed into the passenger seat and waited for Ghost to slip into the driver's side and start the engine. "Anything else from Kevin?"

He shook his head. "No."

"We could stop by there on the way home, if you like."

With a nod, he reversed, turned around and headed down the road to the tavern.

Since it was early on a regular workday, the tavern parking lot was full, with vehicles lining the street, as well.

Charlie suspected they might not get a table as full as it was. But once inside, they waited for only ten minutes before they were seated in a booth near the door.

"Hi, Charlie." Lisa Lambert, a young, bleach-blonde waitress, set a cup in front of Ghost, one in front of Charlie and poured coffee into both. She winked at Lolly. "Juice or chocolate milk?" she asked.

Lolly rocked in her seat. "Chocolate milk!"

After Lisa left, Charlie tried to focus on the menu, when she'd rather stare at the man she'd made love to the night before. When the waitress returned with Lolly's chocolate milk, Charlie still didn't know what she wanted to eat.

"We don't see you in here for breakfast often, Charlie. Who's your fella?"

Charlie's face heated. "He's not—"

Ghost stuck out his hand and smiled at Lisa. "Jon Caspar. Nice to meet you." He leaned close to read her nametag. "Lisa, is it?"

She shook his hand, blushing. "That's right. You

must be new in town. I know I'd remember you, if I'd seen you around."

"I'm not actually. But I'm so much older than you, you wouldn't remember me. I'm back in town for a visit." He reached across the table and laid his hand over Charlie's. "Charlie was good enough to put me up for the week."

"Are you thinking of moving back?" Lisa asked, taking a pad and pen out of her apron pocket.

Charlie's breath caught in her throat and she leaned forward, wanting to hear his answer, even though she knew he was putting on a show for Lisa.

He gave Lisa a friendly smile. "I don't know yet. It depends on the job."

"We're ready to order," Charlie interrupted.

"Oh, right." Lisa pressed her pen to the tablet. "What would you like?"

They placed their orders and Lisa left, her cheeks flushed with color from the smile Ghost gave her before she turned away.

Charlie wanted to smack the grin right off his face. She'd slept with him the night before. How could he flirt with the waitress in front of her?

"Nice one, that Lisa," he said, with a smile playing around his lips. "Why don't I know her?"

Charlie's lips thinned. "Because she was practically in diapers when you were in high school."

He cocked his brows. "Jealous?"

"Not in the least. She's barely out of high school. What use would you have with her? She's not much older than Lolly."

Lolly glanced up from her chocolate milk, her gaze curious.

Ghost's smile faded. "Okay, I'll behave myself, if you'll stop being so serious. Deal?" He held out his hand.

Charlie took his, knowing as soon as they touched, she'd feel that electric shock running through her body. And there it was, searing a path straight to her heart. "Deal."

GHOST DIDN'T KNOW why he'd flirted with the young waitress. He supposed he wanted to get a reaction out of Charlie when she was holding him at arm's length that morning.

He didn't let go of her hand immediately, staring across the table at her. "Just to set the record straight, you're the only woman who interests me."

"For now," Charlie added, trying to pull her hand from his.

He held tight, refusing to release her yet. "For always."

"Please." She finally freed her hand and placed it in her lap, out of his reach. "I find that hard to believe when you haven't been back for seven years."

She was right. He'd tried to forget her in those

seven years, but he'd been unsuccessful. The intensity of his training and deployments had made the time seem to fly. But always in the back of his mind, she was what kept him sane and focused.

The tavern door opened behind Charlie.

Ghost glanced up, his gaze taking in the newcomers entering.

Charlie turned in her seat.

A man in a law enforcement uniform and a woman who appeared to be his wife stepped through the door. They waved at the man behind the counter and were shown to a seat at a table beside Charlie and Ghost's.

Charlie smiled at the man. "Good morning, Sheriff and Mrs. Scott."

The woman smiled. "Good morning, Charlie, Lolly. It's always a pleasure to see you two." She turned to include Ghost in her smile and greeting. "And you are?"

The sheriff nodded, his gaze narrowing on Ghost. "Aren't you Tom Caspar's son?"

Ghost nodded and reached across to shake the sheriff's hand. "Tom is my father."

"Used to be the foreman out at the Dry Gulch Ranch, wasn't he?" the sheriff asked.

"That was him," Ghost said.

"How's he doing down in Florida?"

Ghost grinned. "They love that they haven't had to shovel one scoop of snow since they moved."

The sheriff smiled, nodding. "That's good. Thinking about taking Fran down there for a vacation to see if it's something we'd like for our retirement."

"You should visit my folks," Ghost said. "I'm sure they'd love to see you."

"Might do that." The sheriff turned his attention to the menu.

Lisa returned with three plates of food, setting them in front of Charlie, Ghost and Lolly. "Enjoy," she said and walked away.

The door behind Charlie swung open again with a bang that shook the booth they were sitting in.

Ghost frowned, his gaze following the man who'd entered. He thought he recognized him. His father had met with him on more than one occasion to discuss trading bulls. He'd called him Vanders.

"Sheriff Scott, what are you going to do about the cattle thieves who stole my herd?" the man shouted.

Charlie spun in her seat. "LeRoy?"

He ignored her, his attention on the sheriff. LeRoy Vanders stomped toward the section where the sheriff and his wife sat. He planted his fist on the table and glared at the man.

"LeRoy, we've been over this. You signed on to graze your herd on government property. You read the contract. So, they raised the rates. The contract you signed gives them the right. And it's still cheaper than leasing private property." Sheriff Scott tilted his chin up and narrowed his eyes. "Pay your fees and I'll bet they'll give back your herd."

"My family has been grazing our cattle on that land for over a century. As far as I'm concerned, the government stole that land and is extorting money from me." He pounded his fist on the table.

"What do you expect me to do, LeRoy? You have to take it up with the Bureau of Land Management."

"I expect you to arrest the rustlers who stole my cattle." LeRoy's voice rose. "I was due to take them to the sale. That's the money I use to feed my family and heat my house through the winter. How am I supposed to make do until spring without that money?"

"I can't help you. You have to pay your fees." The sheriff started to rise.

LeRoy pushed him back into his seat and pulled a gun from beneath his jacket.

Mrs. Scott screamed.

Charlie gasped and used her body to block any stray bullets from hitting Lolly.

LeRoy pointed the gun in the air. "I'm tired of being pushed around on my own land. I'm tired of the government taking what belongs to me. I'm tired of the law protecting the criminals and not me and my family."

Ghost eased out of his seat, keeping low, staying out of LeRoy's peripheral vision. He didn't want to startle the man into pulling the trigger. At the angle he was currently holding the gun, LeRoy would put a sizable hole in Ghost if he fired the weapon.

"LeRoy, put down the gun and discuss this like a reasonable man."

"I'll show you reasonable," LeRoy said. Before LeRoy could pull the trigger, Ghost grabbed the man's hand, jerked it into the air and yanked the gun from his grip. Then he twisted the rancher's arm up behind his back.

"Let go of me, damn you!" LeRoy shouted. "Mind your own business. This discussion is between me and the sheriff."

Ghost leaned close to LeRoy's ear. "This discussion stopped being just your business when you pulled the gun." Ghost nodded toward the sheriff. "You want to take him away, or should I?"

A young sheriff's deputy burst through the door. "Got a call from dispatch. Where's the perpetrator?"

The sheriff shook his head. "Over here, Matthews."

Matthews hurried to where Ghost held Mr. Vanders immobile. He snapped the cuffs on the man's wrists and led him toward the exit.

Vanders twisted out of Matthews's grip. "This isn't over by a long shot, Sheriff. I'm not the only one angry about what's going on. You just wait. This isn't the last you'll be hearing from us." He glared at Ghost and Charlie. "And we don't take kindly to interference."

Matthews hooked LeRoy's arm and dragged him out of the door.

Ghost waited until the man was out of the building before he relaxed.

Sheriff Scott held out his hand. "I'll take that. It's evidence."

Ghost gladly handed over the gun.

"Thank you for taking charge," the sheriff said. "I never would have thought Vanders would pull a gun on me. He used to be a reasonable man." He touched his hand to his wife's shoulder. "Are you okay?"

She nodded.

The sheriff sighed. "I'm thinking Florida is looking pretty good about now. How about you, dear?"

Fran pressed a hand to her chest, her face pale, her eyes worried. "People are getting crazy around here. I've never seen them so mad about so much."

A man rose from the table behind the sheriff and shook Sheriff Scott's hand. "You handled that well, Sheriff."

The sheriff frowned. "Should I know you?"

The man smiled. "Randall Gaither. I work with the Apex Pipeline Authority. It's good to see local law enforcement enforcing the laws."

The sheriff's brows twisted. "Just doing my job. Now, if you'll excuse me, I'd like to have breakfast with my wife."

The man nodded. "Of course. Of course." He resumed his seat at the table on the other side of the sheriff and lifted his coffee cup.

Ghost took his seat and stared down at his plate for a moment before he raised his chin and met Charlie's gaze.

Charlie stared at him across the table. "You're as cool as a cucumber." She lifted her glass and her hand shook so much orange juice spilled onto the table. "And I'm shaking like a leaf. You were amazing."

He shrugged. "I was hungry. I figured I wouldn't get to eat my eggs while they were hot, if someone didn't shut him up." He winked at Lolly. "How are your Belgian waffles?"

And just like that, they continued their breakfast as if a man hadn't just pulled a gun in a public place. The less he made of the incident, the better they all were. For Lolly's sake, he didn't let on that he'd been almost as shaken as Charlie. A man had entered the tavern with a gun. He could have started shooting and hurt Charlie or Lolly.

Ghost couldn't let that happen. Wouldn't let it. Hopefully, their problem was solved by the arrest of

LeRoy Vanders. Maybe now, they could relax and enjoy the rest of the week.

He shook his head. Nothing ever was that easy. Hadn't Vanders said he wasn't the only one unhappy about the current state of government in Wyoming? If he was right, he might have been only the tip of the iceberg.

The week ahead didn't look like it was going to be a picnic.

Chapter Nine

"Is today Mother's Day Out?" Lolly asked as they left the tavern.

Charlie had barely been able to choke down her food. After all of the excitement, the patrons of the tavern had either gotten up to leave or stayed to gossip about LeRoy's tirade and Ghost's handling of the situation.

Lisa had been all over Ghost. Forney, the tavern owner, had offered to give them their meal for free.

Ghost had insisted they could pay and did so. He didn't look comfortable with the notoriety. As soon as Lolly finished her meal, he hurried them out the door.

Charlie nodded. "As a matter of fact, today is Mother's Day Out. Would you like to go play at the center?"

"Yes, please. Can I go?" Lolly danced around

Charlie, her eyes wide, her hands pressed together. "Please?"

Charlie glanced over her head at Ghost. "Think it would be okay?"

"Are they inside much of the day?"

"They have arts and crafts and play games in the center."

"It should be okay. We can give the teacher a heads-up to be watchful."

Charlie stared down at her daughter and sighed. The threats had been against her, not her daughter. With LeRoy detained, perhaps the problem had been solved. "Okay," she said to Lolly. "You can go for a couple of hours." It would give her time to meet with Kevin and his computer guy to see if they had anything more to tell them. She was anxious to hear what they found at the address Caveman was supposed to check out that morning.

"Do you remember where the community center is?"

Ghost nodded. "I think so."

"That's where they have the Mother's Day Out. Lolly goes three times a week to play with her friends during the summer." She started to help Lolly up into the truck, but Ghost nudged her aside.

He lifted Lolly, settled her into the booster seat and buckled the seat belt around her.

When he rounded the truck to hold the door for

Charlie, he whispered in her ear. "Are you sure it's a good idea to leave her at the daycare?"

"The threats were against me," Charlie said. "Not Lolly. And she so looks forward to going. I hate to disappoint her." Though she'd had the same misgivings. "How about we let her stay long enough for us to do some digging here in town? We won't be far, if anything happens."

He nodded. "Okay." Ghost helped her up into the truck and climbed into the driver's seat.

The community center was on the edge of town, with a wide, open field used for baseball, soccer and football practice. The center was a converted US Army Armory. The inside was a gymnasium with basketball hoops on either end of the open room. Back when the US Army National Guard occupied the building, they had used the gym for formations on bad weather days and for hip-pocket training in buddy care and field stripping their weapons.

Now the gym was used by locals for the occasional game of basketball and for the Mother's Day Out program, offering the community children a place to play with others their age.

As they drove up to the center, Ghost commented, "Looks better than when I used to come here."

Charlie smiled. "We recently had a Fix It Day. Everyone turned out to paint and do much-needed roof repairs."

"What's with the signs?" He pointed to a grouping of signs outside the center, indicating other businesses besides the community center.

"The city overhauled the old armory offices. The mayor and the county treasurer occupy two of them and the others were rented out to a real estate agent and an insurance salesman. They have access to the outside without going through the gymnasium where the kids play."

Charlie remembered spending a lot of time in the community center as she was growing up. From the annual Halloween parties and Christmas craft shows, to the Fall Festival dances. The community center had been a hub of social gatherings in the Grizzly Pass area.

Ghost parked and helped Lolly out of her seat.

The little girl ran toward the entrance, her face alight with excitement. She had to wait for Charlie to enter the pass code to open the outer door. But once inside, she ran through the front lobby straight into the gym.

Ghost and Charlie followed at a more sedate pace.

Inside, a dozen children were playing four square on the wooden floor of the gymnasium, their shouts echoing off the walls.

Charlie found the woman who ran the Mother's Day Out, her friend from high school, Brenda Larson.

Brenda pushed a stray strand of hair out of her

face and smiled as she weaved through a couple of smaller children to where Charlie and Ghost stood. "Charlie, I'm so glad Lolly was able to come today. Ashley and Chelsea missed her yesterday."

After hugging Charlie, Brenda stood back, her gaze raking over Ghost. She tipped her head, her eyes narrowing. "You look familiar..." Then her face lit. "Jon? Jon Caspar?" She flung her arms around him and hugged his as tightly as she'd hugged Charlie. "You look so much larger than life. You were all buff when you came through several years ago, but look at you." She stood back and ran her gaze over him again. "I barely recognized you. When did you get back in town?"

"Yesterday," he said. "It's good to see you, Brenda."

"What a wonderful surprise." She glanced from Charlie to Ghost and back. "Any special reason you're here?" She paused.

Heat rose up Charlie's neck into her cheeks. "No. Not really. He's here on leave."

Brenda's brows rose again. "Your parents moved south several years ago. I would think you would vacation in Florida with them."

Ghost shrugged. "I haven't been back here in a while. It's nice to be here and explore all of my old stomping grounds."

"I'm sure." Brenda's lips curled up on the corners. "Where are you staying?"

Charlie wasn't up for answering her friend's questions with Ghost standing beside her. "I'm only leaving Lolly for a couple of hours while I run some errands."

Brenda crossed her arms over her chest and nodded. "I see how it is. Ignore the questions and maybe she'll stop asking." She winked at Ghost. "Have it your way." She turned toward the kids. "We're making sock puppets today. I think Lolly will enjoy that. Don't forget we're going on a field trip tomorrow to the Yellowstone Nature Center. You won't want Lolly to miss that. We were able to get an educational grant from the state to fund the bus and the snacks for the trip. If you want to come and help supervise, I'd gladly take all the help I can get."

Charlie frowned. "I'd forgotten that was tomorrow. Lolly's been looking forward to the trip all summer."

"Have her here a few minutes early." Brenda touched her arm. "And don't worry if you can't come along. I know you work from home and it's hard to get away sometimes."

Charlie took Brenda's hand. "About Lolly. Could you keep an extra special close eye on her?"

Brenda glanced toward the happy child, bouncing a ball with three other little girls. "Is she not feeling well?"

Charlie explained the situation with the threats.

"I don't know if she'll become a target because of my meddling."

"Wow." Brenda squeezed her hand. "I'm sorry to hear this is happening to you. I'll be sure to keep her close. We don't plan on leaving the building until after lunch."

"I'll be sure to get her before then."

Brenda's lips twisted as she stared at the little girls. "She'll be disappointed that she won't get to go out on the play set with her pals." Charlie's friend turned back to the adults. "But I understand completely. I'd be leery, as well."

"Thank you, Brenda." Charlie touched her friend's arm.

"We should get together for a girl's night out in Bozeman sometime soon."

"I could use a break," Charlie agreed. "When this mess clears, you're on."

Brenda smiled. "You sure tall, dark and hunky won't mind?"

Charlie glanced up at Ghost. He wouldn't be around when that time came around.

"Whatever makes Charlie happy," Ghost said. His gaze met hers and held it for a long time.

A flash of hope filled Charlie's chest. If Ghost really believed that sentiment, he'd stay in Grizzly Pass with her and Lolly and give up his life with the Navy SEALs. But as much as he loved the path he'd chosen, the likelihood of him leaving it behind was slim to nada.

"Come on, we have some things to check on. And I really do have a job I need to work on. My boss is patient, but he likes it when I meet my project deadlines."

After one last glance in Lolly's direction, Charlie turned toward the door.

Ghost hooked her elbow and walked with her.

The familiarity of his grip on her arm gave her comfort at the same time as it fanned the smoldering embers burning inside. If they didn't have bigger problems to solve, she'd have him take her back to her house to make love to her until it was time to pick up Lolly.

And if wishes were horses...

He handed her up into his truck and closed the door. Then he rounded to the driver's side and climbed in behind the steering wheel. "Where to?"

The first word on the tip of her tongue was *Home*. But she tamped down the urge and answered, "Kevin's. I want to know what they've come up with."

GHOST DROVE BACK to the Blue Moose Tavern and parked in back of the building. Because it was broad daylight, he sent Charlie up first and followed, shortly after.

Garner answered on the first knock. "Come in.

I'm glad you stopped by. And, by the way, thank you for disarming LeRoy before he shot through the ceiling and hit one of us or the computers."

Caveman rose from a chair beside Hack's and held out his hand.

Ghost shook it and nodded toward the computer screens. "Find anything at the physical address for the IP address?"

The D-Force man stretched and shook his head. "Nobody there, only a server and a satellite internet setup. What I gather from the neighbor a half a mile away is that Old Man Huddleston died in his sleep and no one found him until he'd stopped picking up his mail for two weeks."

Garner continued the story. "The mailman notified the sheriff who checked on him and found him in his lounge chair, dead. No one turned off the electricity or gas to the place and someone has been mailing in the payments with cashier's checks."

"The satellite internet is a hack job. Someone with a little know-how is tapped into several satellites. No subscription or paid service."

"Seems like a lot of trouble to keep a social media site up and running."

"And anonymous," Hack said.

"After the demonstration yesterday, I ran into Vanders's wife at the grocery store. She was stocking up on pantry staples, as if she was getting ready for a big snowstorm. I asked her if she'd seen the internet reports about the demonstration. She laughed and said she rarely looked at their computer and didn't know how to use it, anyway."

"That rules out Vanders's wife, but not Vanders himself as the one who'd been leaving threats with Charlie."

"You would think he would have singled me out more at the tavern, if he was angry with me," Charlie pointed out.

"We're still researching Don Sweeney. There's not much on him."

Caveman nodded. "He was the other name I came out of the demonstration with. He's younger and likes to hear himself get loud. He might be in his late twenties. I imagine he knows a little about the internet. Most kids under thirty have been exposed to computers and the internet. Hell, most of them can run circles around me."

Hack turned to face the others. "I found his name on a list of recent layoffs from the Apex Pipeline Authority. I traced him through state birth records. He's the son of a local cattle rancher, Raymond Sweeney, who fell on hard times and had to sell several hundred acres to pay for his wife's cancer treatments. Apparently Don wanted to work on the ranch but had to take a job with the pipeline as soon as he left high school. His mother died last year. Don was laid off this year when the oil prices plummeted."

Ghost narrowed his eyes. "Has he had any run-ins with the law?"

"He had a DUI when he was nineteen, right after his brother died in a farming accident," Hack said, "But other than that, nothing else showed up on his record."

"No tie-in between him and the server setup at the Huddleston place?" Charlie asked.

Caveman rubbed his fist into his opposite palm. "Want me to have a talk with the man?"

"Supposedly, he's up in Montana looking for work in Bozeman."

"Can you verify that?" Charlie asked.

"Already did. His credit card purchases are around the Bozeman area as late as this morning."

Charlie shook her head and drew in a deep breath. "I feel a need for more groceries."

"What?" Ghost shot a glance at her, wondering why the sudden urge to buy more food when she'd been to the store the day before.

A smile tilted Charlie's lips. "Mrs. Penders, one of the owners, is a notorious gossip. If anyone knows anything, she does."

"What are we waiting for?" Ghost turned toward the door.

"*I'm* going. Alone." She gave him a stern look.

"She might clam up with both of us hitting her with questions."

Ghost frowned. "I don't like it when you're out by yourself."

"I've been managing on my own for years," she said.

Taking that punch to the gut, Ghost nodded. "Maybe so, but not with someone threatening your life."

"It's walking distance." She pressed her lips together for a moment before adding, "If you want to walk with me, you can." She held up her finger. "But you're *not* going in."

Caveman, Hack and Garner watched their interchange, their lips twisting.

Heat flooded Ghost's cheeks. He didn't like being told what to do. Still, Charlie didn't belong to him. He had no right to order her around. Even if he and Charlie were a thing, he wouldn't be able to control her. She had a mind of her own.

"She'll be okay," Garner reassured. "And you'll be right outside the store."

"Fine." He turned toward the door. "Let's go."

As they descended the stairs to the ground, Ghost worried. "I don't like leaving you unprotected."

"I'll be fine. I have my gun in my purse."

"You carry?"

"I have since before Lolly was born."

He stared at her. He'd taught her how to shoot a 9 millimeter pistol when he'd been back in town seven years ago. She'd been pretty good, even after only one lesson. "Do you practice?"

"Every chance I get. At the very least, I make it a point to go quarterly. I figure it's no use having a weapon if you don't know how to use it."

Ghost chuckled. "Okay. I feel a little better knowing you can defend yourself."

"And Lolly," she reminded him.

"And Lolly," he agreed. "But it doesn't hurt to have someone covering your six."

"Your six?"

"Navy speak for your six o'clock position," he said with a grin.

"Oh, you mean my back." She smiled. "I like it when you go all military on me. As long as you explain it to me. I don't know much about what you do."

His smile faded. "It's probably just as well. Most of it isn't pretty or something you write home about."

She touched his arm. "I hope someday you'll tell me about why you limp."

"That's easy." He shrugged. "Took shrapnel in my thigh."

She shivered. "You say that like it's no big deal."

"It happens in wartime situations."

"It must be hard to go into battle knowing you or some of your friends might not come out alive."

"Not as hard as thinking about the ones we leave behind. Most SEALs aren't worried about themselves."

"They're worried about their families," she said, finishing his thought. "Is that why you pushed me away when you were setting off for your first assignment as a SEAL?"

They walked along the sidewalk in front of the hardware store, their pace slowing as they neared Penders Grocery.

"I knew what I was getting into would be difficult. I couldn't ask you to wait for me. I'd already heard too many stories about SEALs' wives and girlfriends leaving them when they were on deployment. Some came back to an empty house. Others came back to find other men had taken up residence in their beds."

She stopped short, her hands going to her hips. "And you thought I would do that?"

"No. But other women cracked under the pressure of waiting, not knowing if their men were coming back alive or in a body bag."

"So you decided to spare me the pain?"

He nodded.

"Without giving me the choice." She stared at him a moment longer.

Ghost had left her, convinced he was doing the right thing by letting her live her life without the worry of losing him. Looking at the color in her cheeks, the anger blazing from her eyes, he decided he might have been wrong.

They'd arrived in front of the grocery store.

"Are you sure you don't want me to go in with you? I can keep my distance while you're talking to Mrs. Penders."

She dropped her hands from her hips, inhaled and exhaled before she responded. "I'm quite capable of taking care of myself, and making my own decisions. And have you ever considered that you might need someone back home to cover your six? To be there when you get back and to take care of you when you were wounded?"

He stiffened. "What if I'd lost my leg or an arm? Or hell—what if I came back a paraplegic?"

"You'd still be you where it counts." She touched his chest. "And Lolly would have had a father."

"Lolly has a father. And I want to be a part of her life."

Charlie nodded. "I was wrong to keep her from you, but now isn't the right time to break that to her. We have to figure out who the hell is stirring up trouble. When the dust settles, we'll figure out how to make sure you get to see her." She lifted her chin and stuck her hand out. "Deal?"

He took her hand in his and yanked hard enough to pull her off balance.

Charlie fell into his chest, her hand trapped between them.

"Deal." He pressed a kiss to her lips, taking her mouth with a searing-hot passion he hadn't felt since the last time they'd been together. Whatever happened with the stalker, Ghost refused to walk away from this woman ever again. It had taken him seven years to figure out what was wrong with him, why he felt like he was walking through life with a hole in his chest. He'd been missing a part of himself. The part that was Charlie.

He broke off the kiss, wanting to say so much to her, but the timing wasn't right. Somehow, it never felt right. "Go. Before I say to hell with it and take you back to your house and make crazy love to you."

She stared up at him, her tongue sweeping across her bottom lip. "And that's a bad idea?"

"When someone's after you and we don't know who it is?" He nodded. "Probably not a good idea. See if Mrs. Penders has anything to go on. Find out who has been having trouble besides Vanders."

She cupped his face with her palm. "After all of this, we need to talk."

"Damn right we do," he said. Then he turned her and gave her a gentle nudge toward the store entrance.

Chapter Ten

"Charlie!" Mrs. Penders exclaimed.

Still reeling from Ghost's kiss, Charlie had barely entered the store when the older woman swept her into her arms and hugged her.

"I heard about what happened in the tavern with LeRoy." She stood back and stared at Charlie, running her gaze over her as if searching for injuries or blood. "You're not hurt, are you?"

"No, I'm fine. No bullets were fired. No blood was shed."

"I heard LeRoy went crazy with the sheriff and threatened to shoot him."

Charlie nodded, encouraging the woman to go on about the earlier tussle with the angry Mr. Vanders. "I can't get over how LeRoy behaved toward the sheriff."

"He's just the first rancher in the county to stand up to the law. The man has to be feeling pretty desperate. With his cattle confiscated, he has no way to support his family."

"He said there were others who felt the same. What did he mean by that?" Charlie asked. "Are there more people in the county struggling to make ends meet?"

"Oh, sweetie, there are so many."

"How could I not know this?"

"Most of them keep their troubles to themselves." Mrs. Penders leaned close. "But I hear things as they check out here at the grocery store."

Charlie almost felt guilty for prying into her neighbors' affairs. But it if helped to find Rebecca's attacker and her own stalker, then so be it. "What do you hear?"

"The Parkers are selling their prized, registered quarter horses to pay the mortgage on their place. Because of the increased fees per head of cattle, they aren't making enough off the sale of their steers to keep feeding all of their horses and pay the bills."

"Circle C quarter horses?" Charlie's stomach fell. "They've raised quarter horses for a century."

Mrs. Penders nodded. "I imagine Ryan's grandfather is turning over in his grave. And then there's Bryson Rausch."

"The richest man in the county? I remember his daughter driving a Cadillac convertible to high school. He's having trouble?"

Mrs. Penders nodded, glanced around at the store to make sure no one else was listening. "He bet on the wrong stock in the market and lost everything."

Mr. Rausch had always been very nice to Charlie when she'd run into him in town or at the county fair. Though she'd been envious of his daughter Sierra, she'd always liked Mr. and Mrs. Rausch and hated to know they were in financial trouble.

"Then there's Timothy Cramer," Mrs. Penders went on.

Charlie frowned. "Timothy?"

"Goes by Tim. You might have known his wife, Linnea."

"Oh, yes. Linnea." Her frown deepened. "Her second child died of SIDS not long ago."

Mrs. Penders nodded. "So tragic. It broke Linnea's heart and busted up their marriage."

"That's awful."

"Tim went on a drinking binge and disgraced himself with some floozy in Bozeman. Linnea tried to forgive him, but she couldn't. Not when he didn't even show up for the baby's funeral. She filed for divorce and took half of everything he owned. He's having to sell his grandmother's farm north of town because he can't afford to buy her out. And to add to his misery, he worked as an inspector for the pipeline and lost his job when he was caught falsifying reports.

"The Vanderses and the Parkers aren't the only ones hurting from the increase in range grazing fees. The Mathis family, the Herringtons, Saul Rutherford and the Greenways are all angry with the changes made by the Bureau of Land Management. They can't afford to pay the fees and they can't afford to lease private land. They'll end up selling their cattle at a loss and not having a way to support their families and pay their mortgages next year."

"I'm so sorry to hear that. It makes me sick to know so many are hurting."

"And some are more vocal than others. I wasn't surprised when I heard LeRoy was hauled off to jail. He was a powder keg set to go off. Thankfully someone stopped him from taking others down with him."

"Are there any others as angry and vocal as Mr. Vanders?" Charlie asked.

A customer walked into the store and waved at Mrs. Penders. She waved back and lowered her voice. "Oh, sure. Ernie Martin is angry because the government cut subsidies to his production of angora wool. He's been raising those goats for the past couple of years, making a killing and spending it as fast as he made it. But the money comes from the subsidies, not from the goats or the wool. Now that he's been cut off, he needs it more than ever to make payments on the second mortgage he took out to purchase all of those goats. Ernie's been madder than a hornet about losing the subsidies. He was forced to take a job with the pipeline company, but was laid off when the gas prices dropped. The poor man has had nothing but bad luck."

"Anyone else?" Charlie pushed, knowing she was running out of time with Mrs. Penders. As soon as her customer came to the counter, she'd be interrupted and remember she had a store to run and clean.

"Just about any of those folks who were tagged with bigger grazing right fees. None of them are happy. And they don't know where they'll get the money to pay the fees. Some of them have said they'll stand and defend their herds of cattle from being confiscated by the BLM. Some are willing to die." Mrs. Penders clucked her tongue. "I've never seen people so hot or determined."

"Mrs. Penders. Charlie, what are you ladies doing?" Linnea Cramer stepped up to the counter, carrying a quart of orange juice and carton of eggs. "You two look entirely too intense. What's going on?" Then her eyes widened. "Oh, wait. You have to be talking about the near-shooting at the tavern this morning. Is that it?" Linnea leaned closer. "I heard that you were there when Vanders tried to shoot the sheriff. Someone said Jon Caspar was there and subdued the man. You weren't hurt, were you?"

Charlie smiled and shook her head. "I'm fine. I

feel sorry for Mr. Vanders. He was not happy about his cattle being taken."

"We're all struggling a little from the economy tanking and the oil prices falling. People in this area don't have a lot of choices for jobs. That's why we lose so many young people to the bigger cities."

Mrs. Penders squeezed Charlie's hand. "I was so glad to see you come home to Grizzly Pass."

Charlie's eyes misted as she hugged the older woman. "Mrs. Penders, you're so sweet to say that." She moved away to allow Linnea to reach the counter with her purchases.

"I wish I could say I was happy to be in Grizzly Pass, but I'm not. As soon as my ex-husband sells his property, I'm free to go wherever I choose."

"And where will that be?" Mrs. Penders asked, adding Linnea's grocery items as they spoke.

"I think I'll move to Seattle. At least there I can go to the theater, visit a museum and see the ocean whenever I want."

"I thought you liked it here in Grizzly Pass," Mrs. Penders said.

Linnea's lips thinned. "I did. But things change." She shoved the items across the counter toward Mrs. Penders.

"Is this all?" the store owner asked.

"All I can afford for now," Linnea said.

Mrs. Penders placed the items into bags and

counted out Linnea's change. "I hope things work out for you."

Charlie touched Linnea's arm. "I hope you find the happiness you're searching for."

"Me, too. And the same to you, Charlie. At least, in our daughters, we have someone to love, who loves us unconditionally. Count your blessings. I know I would." She gathered her bags and left the store in a hurry, her eyes suspiciously shiny.

"Poor woman. To lose her second baby and her husband all in less than six months. Thankfully, her first child keeps her grounded." Mrs. Penders transferred her gaze to Charlie. "Here I've been talking all this time. What did you come into the store to get?"

Charlie glanced at the clock on the wall. She'd been there the better part of half an hour. Already it was getting close to lunch and time to collect Lolly. She thought about everything happening in her community, the families falling apart, losing their homes and loved ones. All she wanted to do was gather hers closer. She couldn't wait until her parents were back from their river cruise in Europe. For now, she wanted to spend time with Lolly and Ghost. "I was wondering if you had something I could take out on a picnic. I'm feeling the need to spend time with my family."

Mrs. Penders smile spread across her face. "All of the gloom and doom talk getting to you? You're a smart woman to put your family first." She grabbed Charlie's hand and walked her to the bakery section of the store where she and her husband stocked the glass cases with fresh bread and pastries. "Let me make up some sandwiches and a tub of potato salad and baked beans for you to take with you."

While she waited, Charlie thought about all of the people she knew who had reason to be mad at the world, who might want to take it out on the government. Their list of suspects had grown from one or two to what felt like an entire town. Her heart ached for all of them. But it made it abundantly clear that she, as a mother, needed to focus on what was most important. Her family.

GHOST HAD FOUND a bench in front of the hardware store and settled back to keep an eye on Penders Grocery. In the meantime, he watched as people passed in cars, trucks or on foot. Some stopped to say hello and renew acquaintances with Ghost, taking him for a short stroll down memory lane before they moved on to conduct their business or duck into the tavern for an early lunch.

He'd been there for five minutes when a man around his own age, stopped by and sat next to him. "Heard you were back in town." He held out his hand. "Tim Cramer. You might not remember me. I was a couple years ahead of you in school."

"I remember. You were our star quarterback. You helped the Grizzlies win state that year for the first time in nobody could remember how long."

Tim's lips turned upward on the corners. "That was a long time ago. Back when nothing could stop us." He stared out at Main Street. "What about you? What brings you back to this hellhole?"

"Felt like visiting the place I grew up," Ghost said.

Tim's lip lifted in a half smile bordering on a sneer. "Not someone in particular?"

Ghost shrugged. "Not really." Not at first, anyway. Now that he was there, he wanted to spend all of his time with Charlie and Lolly.

"Didn't you join the Navy?" Tim asked.

Ghost nodded.

Tim glanced his way. "What happened with that?"

"Injury sidelined me."

"Sorry to hear that." He leaned back again. "I hope you're not looking for a job. You'll have to get in line. Half the men in the county are unemployed or barely making it by."

"That's what I'm hearing," Ghost said. "They don't have to worry about me taking their jobs. I won't be here more than a week."

"Yeah, well, enjoy your vacation and tell Charlie hello. See ya around." Tim rose from the bench and walked away, his hands in his pockets.

Ghost remembered Tim as being a lot bigger. Or

was it that Ghost had been a lot smaller, being three
years behind him in high school? The man had been
cordial and friendly, but something about him struck
Ghost wrong. He tried to pinpoint it, but he couldn't.
Soon Charlie emerged from the store with a sack
full of food.

"What did you find out?" he asked.

"Let's go to Garner's loft before we talk." She
crossed the street and stopped at Ghost's truck. He
unlocked it and helped her load the bags into the
back seat.

She led the way up the stairs to where they found
Hack and Garner bent over a computer screen.

"Anything?" Charlie asked.

"We did some digging into LeRoy Vanders's
family. Seems his sons have been in trouble with
the law on more than one occasion. Some of their
arrests include driving under the influence." Hack
read through a report he had up on one of the monitors. "Both Vernon and Dalton have a couple of DUIs
each. Vernon has been arrested on multiple occa-
sions for hunting out of season and poaching on federal land. Dalton has been in several fistfights and
has a restraining order against him. LeRoy's oldest
son did some time in federal penitentiary, for shooting at a law enforcement officer."

Garner nodded toward Charlie. "What did you learn from Mrs. Penders?"

She listed a number of names and circumstances that made the men potential suspects. One jumped out at Ghost.

"Tim Cramer?"

Charlie nodded. "Divorce. He's losing his daughter and half of everything he owns, including the land and house his grandmother left him."

"I spoke with him while waiting for you to come out of the store."

Charlie's eyes narrowed. "What did he say?"

Ghost shrugged. "Nothing incriminating. He asked if I was looking for work and told me I'd have to get in line since half the men in the county were unemployed. He also told me to say hello to you." He captured Charlie's gaze. "I couldn't read anything into what he said."

"I ran into his ex-wife in the store. Was he watching for her to come out, do you think?"

"Was that the woman who came out before you did?"

"Yes."

"No, he was gone before she emerged."

"We'll look into his background and see if we can come up with anything." Garner half sat on the edge of a table, his leg dangling over. "I feel like we're searching for the needle in the haystack."

"I checked the Vanderses' utility bills," Hack said. "They have a phone line and internet. They are all on the same plan. They might be involved in whatever takeover they're planning, but we don't know if it's one of them, or all of them. And we don't know if they are computer savvy enough to tap into Charlie's webcam. That takes more sophistication and technical knowledge."

"Check Cramer, Rausch and Parker," Charlie said. "Any one of them would have to be computer savvy to do their business. Raising prized horses would require a website and email in these times. A man who makes and loses his wealth in the stock market is heavily involved with technology. And a man working for the pipeline as an inspector has to have the ability to communicate using modern technology."

"On it," Hack said.

"In the meantime, we're heading out to lunch," Charlie said.

Ghost shot a glance her way. "We are?"

She nodded. "After we pick up Lolly."

As they descended the stairs, he asked, "Where are we going for lunch?"

She responded, "Out."

Ghost wasn't sure he liked the vague answer, but

he went with it. "Just promise me we're not going into the lion's den."

She shot a sideways glance at him. "Huh?"

"You know. We're not taking Lolly into a potentially dangerous location where crazy men wield guns."

Her lips twitched and a smile spread across her face.

Ghost swallowed hard on the constriction in his throat. This was the Charlie he remembered from seven years ago. Happy, carefree and in love with life.

"Uh, Ghost, we've already done that today. You remember. The tavern?"

He would have laughed at her teasing, but the thought of LeRoy Vanders shooting that gun inside the restaurant where Lolly and Charlie were close enough to be killed with a single bullet made his chest hurt. "Yeah."

She was right, but it wasn't funny.

Lolly was in the middle of playing hopscotch with her girlfriends when they arrived. She dragged her feet, her bottom lip sticking out just a little. "Can I stay longer?"

"No, sweetheart," Charlie said, taking her daughter's hand. "But I have a special surprise I think you'll like."

Lolly's face perked and she hopped up and down. "What is it?"

"My question, exactly," Ghost muttered.

"Now, it wouldn't be a surprise if I told you, would it?" Charlie winked at Lolly and lifted her chin when she glanced toward Ghost.

He liked this teasing, fun Charlie. She didn't seem as weighted by responsibility. She appeared to be making an effort to include them in the fun.

Ghost went along with her. "Come on, sugar bear." He swung Lolly up in his arms and carried her toward the truck. "The sooner we get going, the sooner we discover what this big surprise is."

Minutes later they were on the road heading toward Charlie's house.

As Ghost neared the turn, Charlie put her hand on his arm. "Keep going."

"Where to?" he asked.

"I think you'll know when you get there." She sat back in her seat. "Follow the highway heading south out of town."

He increased his speed as he left the town limits and hit the open road. Before long, his instincts knew where they were going without Charlie telling him. "We're going to the Dry Gulch Ranch, aren't we?"

She smiled.

His chest tightened, his mind filling with memories of growing up on the Dry Gulch Ranch. Five generations of Whitakers had owned the ranch. Ghost's father had worked for the fourth of the five. Ghost had grown up with Trace Whitaker, riding horses, swimming in the creek, hunting and fishing on the Dry Gulch. They'd been best friends even though his father had worked for Trace's father.

"Has Trace returned from his stint in the Army?" Ghost asked.

"Not yet. But the foreman is aware we're coming out and Trace left word with him that you're welcome to have run of the ranch anytime you're home on leave."

"I haven't been back since my parents moved away."

"It hasn't changed a whole lot. I came out once to help the foreman's wife set up her new computer."

Ghost focused his attention on maneuvering through the huge gate with the cattle guard over the road. Then he drank in the view leading up to the first place he'd ever called home. The winding drive through pastures with the mountains as a backdrop was forever seared into his memory.

He rolled down the window to smell the scent of the pinion pines as he neared the ranch housing compound. The drive wove through a stand of trees. At the last curve, the trees seemed to part and the big rock-and-cedar house with the wide porches and huge expanses of windows appeared.

To Ghost, it felt like coming home. He turned before he reached the house and drove around to the back where the foreman's quarters sat near the huge old barn.

Charlie had been right. Nothing much had changed, except one major item. His parents wouldn't be there to welcome him and he wasn't home. This was another foreman's lodgings now.

Still, the surprise was one he could enjoy anyway.

Jonesy, the wiry cowboy with salt-and-pepper hair who'd taken over from Ghost's father, met them in front of the barn with a friendly smile.

Charlie helped Lolly out of the truck while Ghost went to greet the older man.

"Jon Caspar, you're a sight for sore eyes." Jonesy had been one of the ranch hands Ghost's father had trained to take over his position as foreman. He'd been there as Ghost was growing up on the ranch.

Ghost engulfed the man in a hug. "How are you and Mrs. Jones?"

"The missus is doing fine. She would have been here, but she's in Bozeman picking up some ranch supplies and some fabric for her quilting bee or some such nonsense." He stepped back and looked at Ghost. "You look great. The Navy must be treating you right." His smile slipped. "Heard you were injured." He tilted his head from side to side, his gaze skimming over Ghost. "Nothing permanent, I hope."

Ghost laid a hand on his leg. "Took a bit of shrapnel to the thigh. I'll be okay." He didn't go into the detail of how long the doctors spent in the operating room removing all of the shards of metal and reattaching major veins. Or the physical therapy it took to get him back to where he was, standing on his own two feet, with only a limp.

He knew he still had a long way to go before they would allow him to return to his unit. Hell, he still had to face the Medical Review Board. They might decide to medically retire him. He refused to think of that now. Not when the sun was shining and he could smell the hay in the barn and the earthy scent of horse manure.

"I saddled a couple of horses and a pony for your ride. I think you'll like the ones I picked." Jonesy's brows drew down. "I didn't think about it, but can you ride with your injury?"

Ghost wasn't sure. "I'll let you know after I've given it a try."

"I gave you a gentle gelding, and Charlie has one of our sweetest-tempered mares."

"What about me?" Lolly asked, her eyes wide, excited.

Jonesy bent to Lolly's level. "You get to ride Annabelle, a rescue pony Mr. Whitaker insisted on giving a home. She's just the right size for a little girl like you." He straightened and gave Charlie a direct look. "Annabelle is very well trained and will behave herself with the little one."

Charlie smiled. "I know you wouldn't give Lolly anything she couldn't handle. She's been taking riding lessons at the Red Wagon Stables on the other side of town, so she knows a little bit about sitting in the saddle and handling the reins."

"That's great. You can't start them too young. If you ever want to come ride, you can come out here. Mr. Whitaker would like knowing his horses are getting some exercise besides what me and the missus are giving them."

Charlie shifted the bag she carried into one arm and hugged the man with the other. "Thank you, Jonesy. It's good to see you. I don't get out here nearly enough." She glanced down at what she was carrying. "I brought the food for a picnic. I don't suppose you have an old blanket and some saddlebags?"

"A picnic?" Lolly clapped her hands. "We're going on a picnic."

"When you called to tell me what you wanted to do, I got things ready for you. The saddlebags are on Jon's horse and the blanket is tied to the back of yours."

"Thank you." Charlie kissed the older man's cheek.

A moment later, Jonesy brought out the horses and the pony and tied them to a hitching post.

Ghost helped Charlie put the food in the saddle-bags and then he stood at the ready while Lolly mounted the chocolate brown pony with the cream-colored mane and tail. Annabelle stood patiently while Lolly settled into the saddle.

Jonesy adjusted the stirrups to fit her legs and handed her the reins. "If you tap her gently with your heels, she'll walk. Pull back on the reins when you want her to stop."

"I learned this at my lesson," Lolly said. She tapped her heels and the pony moved forward.

Lolly's grin filled Ghost's heart with joy. He'd never thought about children of his own, but deep down, he'd wanted them, and he'd wanted his children to ride horses and have a love of the outdoors.

Ghost held the mare's head while Charlie mounted. Then he approached the gelding, praying he could hoist himself into the saddle. Thankfully, it was his right leg that had been damaged the most. He set his boot in the stirrup and swung his leg over. So far, so good. He had trouble setting his right foot in the stirrup, but eventually managed. "Where to?"

Charlie shook her head. "You know the ranch better than I do. Lead the way."

Jonesy opened the pasture gate for them and waited as Charlie and Lolly passed through. When Ghost rode abreast of him, he leaned toward him.

"Take them to the pool in the creek where you and Trace used to swim. That's about the prettiest place on all of the ranch."

Ghost nodded. "You're right. I will."

Jonesy glanced up at the clear blue sky. "The weatherman calls for rain this afternoon."

"We'll be back before then," Ghost said.

"If you get caught up on the mountain—"

"I know of a place we can hole up until we can get down."

Jonesy smiled and nodded. "You should. You spent most of your youth in those hills." His smile faded. "Keep an eye out for bears. I've seen bear scat and claw marks on trees out that direction. They're around."

"Will do," Ghost promised.

Jonesy closed the gate behind them and headed back to the barn.

Ghost nudged the gelding into an easy trot to catch up with the others. When they came abreast, he was glad when the horse settled into a steady walk. The constant jolt of a trot was too hard on his recovering leg.

The three of them ambled across the pasture, their pace set by the pony.

Ghost pointed to wildflowers and trees, naming them for Lolly. She asked questions, curious about the birds and the ground squirrels they saw along the way. They spied antelope in the distance and admired a bald eagle flying overhead.

By the time they arrived at the creek pool it was well past lunchtime. As soon as they tied the horses to the bushes, they worked to spread the blanket over the grass and set out the food Mrs. Penders had prepared for their picnic.

Ghost ate in silence, enjoying the sounds of the birds and the rustle of leaves as a gentle breeze rippled through the branches. When they finished, they packed the leftover food in the saddlebag and set it aside.

Charlie stretched out on the blanket, her arms crossed behind her head, a smile lifting the corners of her lips.

Lolly played nearby, skipping stones in the pool.

Ghost leaned up on one elbow, his gaze on Charlie, Lolly in his peripheral vision. "I understand why my parents moved to Florida, but I can't help thinking that this is as close to heaven as you can get."

She closed her eyes, her smile widening. "I thought you might like to get away from town for a little while."

"What made you think of coming here?"

Her smile slipped as she looked up at him. "After listening to Mrs. Penders talking about all the troubles people were having, I needed a pick-me-up, and I figured you could use one, too. Life's too short to go around looking for what's wrong with it. If you just open your eyes, you can see the beauty all around you."

Ghost nodded, soaking in the beauty that was Charlie. "I agree."

"Seriously, look around us. Have you seen anything more beautiful?"

"Never."

She turned toward him. "You're not looking at the trees and the sky."

"No. I'm not." He touched her cheek with the back of his knuckles. Her skin was as soft and smooth as it had been seven years ago. And her lips… He bent to taste them.

She didn't resist. Instead, she opened to him and met his tongue with her own in a long, languid caress that stirred his blood and made his heart beat faster.

Eventually, he lifted his head to stare down at her.

"Remember the last time we were here?" she asked, cupping his cheek with her palm.

He nodded. "We skinny-dipped in the pool."

She smiled. "Uh-huh. I think this is where Lolly was conceived."

He shook his head, his heart full to bursting. He

glanced across at Lolly, the beautiful little girl with hair as fiery as her mother's.

A movement behind the child made Ghost refocus his attention on the dark brown woolly mass on the other side of the pool, rearing up on its hind legs.

Grizzly!

Chapter Eleven

Ghost lurched to his feet. "Lolly," he said, his voice low and urgent. "Lolly," he said a little louder.

She was bending over picking flowers.

Charlie rolled to her feet and stared in the direction Ghost was looking. Her gasp indicated she'd seen what he was looking at. She started forward, but Ghost put out a hand to stop her. "Get to the horses and be ready to mount with Lolly. I'm going to distract the bear while you two get away."

"You can't run on that leg. I should distract her while you and Lolly get away."

"Just do it," he said, his voice low, his tone unbending.

Charlie left the blanket and the saddlebag and eased toward the horses, quickly untying them from the bushes.

Lolly had yet to see the grizzly. She glanced

up and looked in Ghost's direction. "Aren't these pretty?" she called out.

Ghost froze, his gaze on the grizzly across the pool from Lolly. Then he saw movement in the brush behind the big bear. Two cubs emerged.

Holy hell. It was a mama grizzly and her two cubs. Lolly was in mortal danger.

"Lolly, look at me," Ghost said. He bent to gather the saddlebag and blanket. "Sweetheart, go to the horses." In a commanding tone, he said, "Now."

She frowned, looked down at the flowers and back up at him, "But—"

"Now," he repeated swinging wide, away from Lolly toward the narrower end of the pool. If the grizzly charged, it would be slowed by the deeper water. In which case, Lolly would have time to run to the horses. Hopefully, Charlie would get her in the saddle and the hell out of there before the grizzly cleared the pool.

If the bear was smart enough to go around to the shallow end, she'd focus her ire on Ghost and he'd use the saddlebag and the blanket as distractors to give himself time to get away.

That was the plan and the backup plan. It was up to the bear to make the first move.

Lolly frowned and started toward the horses.

The grizzly mama roared and ran into the water.

Lolly spun toward the sound, saw the grizzly and screamed.

"Run!" Ghost yelled.

"Run, Lolly!" Charlie said. She had the horses' reins in her hands. They'd spotted the grizzly and were dancing backward, pulling her away from Lolly.

The girl seemed to be frozen for a moment. Then she dropped the flowers, turned and ran as fast as her little feet could carry her, straight for her mother.

The grizzly started into the water. When it got too deep, she changed direction toward the shallow, narrow end where Ghost was waiting. He waved the blanket, catching her attention.

The bear roared again and ran toward him.

Ghost took off, pain shooting through his bum leg. Too late, he remembered he wasn't as agile as he used to be. He sure as hell couldn't outrun a grizzly. His only hope was to fool her into attacking the blanket while he climbed a tree. He wasn't fool enough to believe she wouldn't climb up after him, so he'd have to make the blanket convincing enough to keep her occupied while he made good his escape.

The mama bear roared again and charged out of the deeper water toward him.

Ghost ran for the brush. As he passed a big bush, he lifted the blanket letting it catch the wind enough to spread it out, then he laid it down over a tall bush and ran behind it.

Moving from bush to bush, he ran as fast as he could, careful not to let the grizzly see him. When he reached a tree he thought he could climb, he popped his head above the bushes enough to locate the grizzly.

She was mad, slapping at the blanket and the bushes with her murderous claws. Once she'd ripped the blanket to shreds, she reared up on her hind legs again and gave another terrifying roar.

Ghost eased himself up into the tree, reaching only for the branches on the far side of the thick trunk. Several times he leaned around the side to spy the grizzly sniffing through the bushes, trying to find him.

He kept climbing, higher and higher. The narrower the branches, the less likely the grizzly could reach him. Despite common misconception, he knew grizzlies could climb trees. It was harder for them than for the black bears, because of their giant claws, but they could climb. His best bet was not to draw attention to himself.

When he'd gone as high as he could, he stopped and remained absolutely still.

The bear kept coming, her nose to the ground, sniffing for him. When she reached the base of the big tree, she circled it several times, sniffing and looking up into the branches.

Ghost held his breath, praying she didn't see him and hoping Charlie and Lolly had gotten far enough away that the grizzly couldn't easily catch up to them.

Several minutes crept by. The bear reared on her back legs and hugged the base of the tree. For a heart-stopping moment, Ghost thought she would climb.

Then the sound of a cub calling out in the woods came to him and the grizzly at the same time.

For a moment, she continued to stare up into the branches of the tree. With one last roar, she dropped to all fours and hurried toward the sounds of her cubs.

Ghost watched her until he couldn't see her anymore. Then he gave it another two or three minutes before he eased his way down through the branches. As he got close to the ground, he paused, took a moment to scan the area. When he was absolutely positive the bear had gone, he slipped to the ground and crept through the woods, making his way toward the pool. The grizzly and her cubs had moved on.

Ghost walked back along the trail they had arrived on earlier, hoping to catch up to Charlie and Lolly. His leg ached and the clouds had settled in over the hills.

Soon fat drops splattered on the ground and in his

face. Part of him hoped Charlie and Lolly had gone back to the barn. Another part hoped they were just ahead of him on the trail.

The drops turned to a deluge of cold rain soaking through his clothes, chilling him to the bone.

He was wiping his eyes for the tenth time when he glanced up to see dark masses blocking the trail ahead. For a moment his heart skipped several beats. His first thoughts were of the bear and her cubs. Then he could make out the shapes of two horses and a pony, a woman leading them and a little girl huddled close to her mother's legs.

Limping faster, Ghost hurried toward them. "Charlie! Lolly!"

They turned as one and ran toward him, flinging their arms around him.

"We were so scared," Lolly said, her words coming out on a sob.

"Are you all right?" Charlie asked, rain streaming down her face. She leaned back and studied him, her gaze going over him from head to foot.

"I'm fine. I don't think I've climbed a tree that fast since I was a kid." He grinned and lifted Lolly into his arms. "Come on, I know of a hunting cabin close by. We can take shelter until the storm passes."

He settled Lolly on the pony, helped Charlie into her saddle and pulled himself up onto his horse.

Within a few minutes, he'd found the cabin they'd used during the fall hunting season, years ago. The door opened easily and the inside was dry, even if it wasn't warm. Fortunately, someone had stacked dry cordwood next to the potbellied stove. Matches and tinder were right where they had always been. Soon Ghost had a fire going and the interior of the cabin grew cozy warm.

The one-room structure had two twin beds, the thin mattresses folded over to keep the dust from settling on the surface.

Charlie stood at the window, staring out at the rain coming down. "It doesn't look like it will let up soon and it'll be getting dark soon."

Ghost removed his soaked shirt and hung it on a nail on the wall, close to the stove. "We might as well get comfortable. Looks like we'll be spending the night."

Lolly sat on one of the two chairs, her eyes wide. "Will the bear find us here?"

"No, sweetheart," Charlie reassured her.

"If she does, will she break down the door?" Lolly shivered.

"You'll be okay here in the cabin," Charlie said. "She only chased us because she was protecting her babies."

"I'm scared," Lolly whispered, a violent shiver shaking her body.

Charlie smoothed a hand over her daughter's damp head. "You know what I do when I'm scared?"

Lolly shook her head.

"I get busy." She drew Lolly to her feet. "Let's get these beds ready to sleep in."

Ghost pitched in to help them shake the dust from the mattresses. They found sleeping bags rolled up in an airtight plastic container in one of the corners. On one of the shelves they found cans of beans and corned beef and hash. Another shelf contained a pot and an old, manual can opener. Soon, they had dinner of beans and corned beef and hash.

Charlie stripped Lolly out of her damp clothing and tucked her into a sleeping bag. She hung the items near the stove to dry.

With the warmth of the fire, a full belly and the people he loved surrounding him, Ghost couldn't think of a place he'd rather be.

Could he have a different life than that of a SEAL? Was he ready to leave it to the younger, more agile men coming out of BUD/S training?

He looked around at the small cabin, tucked away from the world and realized this was his world. These were the people he cared most about. He wasn't sure of what he'd do career-wise, but he would take into account the need to be with his daughter. If Charlie gave him a second chance, he'd spend the rest of his life making up to her for the past seven years.

CHARLIE ARRANGED THE sleeping bags over the thin mattresses and settled Lolly into one of the small beds.

Lolly reached out for her mother's hand. "Will you sleep with me?"

"You bet." Charlie had already decided the beds were too small for her to sleep with Ghost. With Lolly in the same room, she didn't think it right for her to be in bed with a man who was more or less a stranger to her daughter.

She lay down beside Lolly, pulled her close and sang the soft ballad she'd sung to her daughter since she was a tiny baby.

Ghost settled in the bed beside them and turned on his side, his gaze on her and his daughter.

Soon, Lolly's breathing grew deeper and her body went limp. With her hand tucked beneath her cheek, she slept.

Charlie stared past her to the man who'd risked his life to save them from being mauled by a grizzly. With an injured leg, he'd run through the woods, providing a sufficient distraction for them to get away.

Her heart squeezed hard in her chest like it had when she'd ridden away with Lolly, not knowing if he would escape the bear. For all Charlie knew, Ghost might have been killed or wounded so badly, he could have been lying on the ground bleeding to death.

She and Lolly had ridden hard, putting half a mile distance between them and the pool where the grizzly had appeared.

About that time, the clouds lowered on them. It began to drizzle and Charlie couldn't go any farther without knowing. She'd turned back the way they'd come, determined to find Ghost. Lolly had been just as worried about him, insisting they go back.

The sky had opened up, dumping rain on them. They couldn't see ahead and the horses slipped on the trail. She'd gotten down from the saddle and set Lolly down beside her. If Ghost was to be found, she had to be close enough to the ground to see him.

When he'd emerged from the deluge, walking toward them, Charlie's heart had nearly exploded with the joy she'd felt.

She and Lolly had run to him, hugging him close. At that moment, Charlie knew she was still hopelessly and irreversibly in love with the man.

And she'd been terribly wrong to keep news of his daughter from him.

"I'm sorry," she whispered, capturing his gaze in the soft glow coming from the potbellied stove.

His brows dipped. "For what?"

She smoothed a hand over her daughter's drying hair. "For keeping Lolly from you."

"I didn't make it easy for you to come out and tell

me," he said. "I'm sorry I was so selfish when I left, that I didn't consider what I was leaving behind."

"You were just starting your career. You didn't need to be saddled with the worry of a family."

"And you shouldn't have had to go it alone with a child to care for."

"We made mistakes," Charlie said.

"The question is, do we continue to make the same mistakes, or do we make things right?"

His words were softly spoken, but they were heavy, weighing on Charlie's mind. "You still have a career with the military. I can make sure you see Lolly on holidays."

"I want to be with her more than that."

Charlie's gut clenched and her breath caught in her throat. Was he going to sue for custody? God knew he had a right to.

"Being back...being with you...makes me want more." He swung his legs over the side of the little cot and winced. "Being a SEAL used to be every-thing to me. The training I went through made me want to prove something to my team and to my-self. But after the first year or two, I realized there will always be another battle and another enemy to fight. I didn't think it would be right to bring some-one else into my personal life, when my life wasn't guaranteed."

"Nobody's life is guaranteed," Charlie argued. "I

could be hit by a bus tomorrow. Or worse, we could be targeted by homegrown terrorists. You can't live thinking about what *could* happen. You have to muddle through with what you know and what you have."

"I know that, but a SEAL's life expectancy is a hell of a lot lower than most people's. It wouldn't be fair to subject a loved one to the constant worry."

Charlie stiffened, the heat of anger rising in her chest. "So you make that determination unilaterally? Have you ever thought it isn't fair to exclude a loved one from the decision?"

His lips twisted. "I thought it was the right decision."

"Well, you might be the only one who thought it. If you bothered to include all involved in the decision-making process, you might have come to an alternate conclusion."

Charlie flipped over onto her other side. Her eyes stung and she swallowed hard. She wouldn't cry another tear for Ghost. The man could be so thickheaded. The way he was thinking would doom them to the same mistake they'd made seven years ago. When would he ever learn?

With a child to care for and protect, she couldn't spend her days mooning over a man who couldn't commit.

"Charlie, I've never stopped loving you," he said.

"Yeah, yeah," she muttered, without turning over.

"You have a funny way of showing it." The last of her words came out garbled as she choked back a sob.

"Please don't turn away from me," he said.

"I have a job, Lolly has plans for tomorrow and I need sleep. I have two lives to think of. Figure out your own life."

"But—"

"Please," she whispered. "Just leave me alone. I'm too tired to think or argue."

"We're not through with this conversation," he said, his tone firm.

She lay silent, tears slipping down her cheeks. She refused to sniffle. He couldn't know that he was breaking her heart all over again.

Charlie lay awake, pretending to be asleep long after Ghost settled back in his bed.

She hurt so much it was a physical pain she couldn't ignore. Before the sun rose, she was up, looking out the window at the gray light of predawn.

"How long have you been awake?" Ghost whispered.

"Not very." She didn't face him. She couldn't. Her heart weighed heavily in her chest and one little word from the man she loved and she might burst into tears.

"I'm hungry," Lolly said. She stretched in the bed

and rubbed her knuckles against her eyelids. "Are we going home?"

"As soon as you get your clothes and boots on, we can start back," Charlie said.

Lolly rolled out of bed and dressed in her dry clothing and then pulled on her pink cowboy boots. "My boots are still wet."

"We'll get you into some dry clothes and shoes when we get back home."

"And breakfast?" Lolly asked.

"And breakfast." Charlie forced a smile to her lips and turned in Lolly's direction. "Ready?"

Ghost had his boots on and had tucked his shirt into his waistband. Without saying a word, he left the little cabin, gathered the horses and waited for Charlie and Lolly to mount before he swung up onto his horse.

They rode down the mountain as the sun edged over the horizon.

Charlie's gaze scanned the hillside and the brush for grizzlies, not wanting a repeat of their encounter from the day before. The ride remained blissfully uneventful.

Jonesy greeted them at the barn, leading a saddled horse, his brows furrowed. "I was just about to ride out to find you three."

"We had a grizzly sighting and got caught in the rain," Ghost informed the man.

Jonesy shook his head. "I'd noticed bear scat in that area, but I'd hoped you wouldn't run into one."

"It was a mama and her two cubs," Lolly said. "She didn't like it that we were around."

"Glad you got away without injury. Some aren't as fortunate." Jonesy grinned. "Did you stay in the hunting cabin?"

Ghost nodded. "I'll bring some canned goods and firewood to replenish what we used."

"No, don't do that. I was going to run some up this week anyway. Glad you found dry wood and something to eat."

"We are, too," Charlie said. "Otherwise it would have been a much more uncomfortable night." She slid out of her saddle and started to lead the horse into the barn.

"I'll take care of the horses. You three look like you could stand some breakfast. The missus has extra scrambled eggs if you're hungry."

"I'm hungry," Lolly exclaimed.

"Are you sure it's not a bother?" Charlie asked.

"She'd be happy to have someone to fuss over," Jonesy reassured her.

"We can't stay long," Charlie glanced down at Lolly. "Today is the day for the field trip to Yellowstone National Park. We have to be there early."

"I'll hurry," Lolly promised.

They made their way to the foreman's little cottage where Mrs. Jones had breakfast waiting on the table.

"How did you know we were coming?" Lolly asked.

Mrs. Jones blushed. "I was watching through the window."

"We don't want to burden you," Ghost said.

She waved her hands. "It was no trouble at all. We get so few visitors, it's a pleasure to cook for someone else."

Ghost, Charlie and Lolly took seats at the table and dug into the scrambled eggs and thick slices of ham Mrs. Jones served.

Charlie hadn't felt much like eating, but the ham and eggs hit the spot and helped lift her flagging spirits. By the time she left the Dry Gulch Ranch, she was resigned to whatever happened.

Lolly's chatter filled the silence on the drive home.

While Lolly took a quick shower, Charlie changed into dry clothes and shoes, washed her face and brushed her hair back into a ponytail. She'd considered wearing makeup, but decided it was too late to impress a man who wasn't going to stick around. Resigned to going without makeup, she ducked into her office and powered up her computer. Once the monitor flashed to life, she clicked on the URL of the Free America group and scrolled through the messages. She'd just about reached the bottom when Lolly called out.

"I'm ready." Her daughter entered her office wearing jeans and her community center T-shirt and sneakers.

"You were fast," Charlie remarked. She glanced at the computer one last time and frowned.

A message popped up on the group that caught her attention.

Let it begin with a meeting of the mines

A chill slithered down Charlie's spine as she turned toward Lolly. The message wasn't directed at her, this time. It was directed toward the Free America group. So much for assuming LeRoy Vanders was the leader. He was safely in jail with no access to the internet.

Though Charlie wasn't sure what the message meant, one thing was certain, something was about to start. What, she didn't know.

"Come on, Mommy. We're going to be late and miss the trip." Lolly spun on her heels and ran down the hallway.

Charlie rose and met Ghost by the front door where he held Lolly's hand.

What did it mean? Had they meant to spell mines or had it been a misspelling intended to be minds?

The hills were dotted with abandoned mines from the gold rush era. "Ready?" Charlie asked, her mind on the message, her stomach churning.

"Yes!" Lolly jumped up and down. "We're going to Yellowstone today. We get to ride on a bus."

Her excitement brought a small smile to Charlie's lips. As she gathered her keys and purse from the hallway table, the phone next to them rang.

Charlie froze, almost afraid to answer. Would it be another harbinger of potential doom? She lifted the phone from the charger. "Hello."

"Charlie, Kevin here."

"Hey, Kevin," she said. "What's up?"

"We have some satellite images that might interest you and Ghost."

Her gaze met Ghost's and a tremor of awareness rippled through her. "We're on our way to town. I have to drop off my daughter at the community center, then we'll be there."

"See you in a few, then." Garner ended the call.

Ghost met her gaze with a question in his eyes.

"He has some satellite images he wants us to look at." She looped her purse over her shoulder and followed Ghost and Lolly outside.

"We can take my Jeep. I feel like driving." She might as well get used to being that single parent again. It wouldn't be long before Ghost left.

Ghost didn't argue, but moved the booster seat

from his truck into the backseat of her Jeep and buckled Lolly in.

Once again, Lolly jabbered away. If the adults weren't responding, the little girl was too excited about riding in the bus to notice.

As they neared town, Charlie pulled up in front of the tavern first. "Why don't you get started reviewing the images? I'll be back in less than five minutes."

"I can wait," he said, not budging from the passenger seat.

"Please," she said, staring straight out the front window without looking into his eyes. "I need just a few minutes alone."

He hesitated.

In her peripheral vision she could see his jaw harden and his lips press into a thin line. Then he leaned into the backseat and chucked Lolly beneath her chin. "Have a great time at Yellowstone. Don't pet any bison while you're there."

"Don't be silly. Bison are wild animals," she said.

He climbed out of the Jeep and stood on the sidewalk watching as they drove away.

Charlie felt as if she was leaving him for good, knowing perfectly well she'd be back to study satellite images. But she couldn't help looking at him in the rearview mirror. He looked so sad, and that made her heart hurt even more.

What were they going to do? How could they fix a relationship that wasn't meant to be?

More immediately, she worried about the message.

Let it begin with a meeting of the mines.

Chapter Twelve

Ghost wanted to kick himself. Hard. Last night he could have made things right with Charlie. He could have told her he loved her and wanted to be with her more than he wanted to breathe. Instead, he'd fumbled the pitch and struck out.

She'd dropped him off like she wanted nothing to do with him. If he didn't know better, he'd bet she didn't come back to view the images Garner's team had come up with.

And then there were the threats against Charlie that had him worried. She ran around town without him as if no one would attempt to harm her. And maybe no one would, but that didn't make Ghost any more confident. He had half a mind to jog down to the community center and make sure she was all right. It was only a few blocks. But wait. He wasn't quite up to jogging. Not without a whole lot of pain.

He didn't believe LeRoy Vanders was the one

posting the threats. Frankly, the man didn't seem technologically advanced enough to track her back to her webcam. But if not Vanders, then who?

Yeah, he was being foolish. Instead of following her, he climbed the stairs to Garner's office and knocked.

Caveman opened the door. "Good, you're here. You'll want to see this." He stepped aside.

Garner, Caveman and Hawkeye stood at the large monitor mounted on the wall, staring at a satellite image.

Garner glanced over his shoulder. "Ghost, glad you made it. Where's Charlie?"

"She went on to the community center. She'll be here in five minutes."

"Do you want us to wait until she gets here to go over what we found?"

"No, she said to get started without her." Ghost stepped up beside Garner. "What's this a picture of?"

"The mountain between Grizzly Pass and the highway turnoff that leads to Yellowstone National Park. The image is from a week ago." Most of the mountain was dark and dense with lodgepole pine trees. Garner pointed to a place that appeared to be a gash in the landscape. "See this?"

"Looks like an old mining camp," Ghost noted.

"It is. We looked it up. It's the abandoned Lucky

Lou's Gold Mine. It played out about forty years ago and has been closed since." Garner glanced back at Hack. "Show two nights ago."

Hack clicked his mouse and the screen in front of the others flickered. For a moment, it appeared unchanged. Until Ghost leaned closer and noticed a change in the mine area.

"Are those vehicles?"

Garner nodded. "We counted half a dozen. And if you look here at that bright dot, we think that's a campfire, and next to it are people. Show the infrared shot," he called out.

Hack clicked and another image appeared with green spots of color. Where the campfire had been was brighter, almost white.

Garner pointed to several smaller dots of green lined up from the back of one vehicle to the side of a hill. "Why would they be lined up at the back of one of the vehicles and all the way to the mine entrance?"

"Are they unloading something?" Ghost asked.

Garner nodded. "That's the only thing we could think of. Caveman, Hawkeye and I are headed out this morning to check on it."

"I want to go," Ghost said.

"Do you think Charlie will be okay without you to keep an eye on her?"

Ghost wrestled with his desire to go with her and

his desire to find out what someone was storing in an old mine in the middle of the night. "I'd better stay."

The phone rang in Kevin's office.

Hack lifted it. "Yeah." A moment later, he held it up. "It's for you, Kevin."

The DHS team leader grabbed the phone. "Kevin, here." He listened for a moment and nodded. "Are you sure you'll be all right?" He paused. "Okay. I'll tell him." The man handed the phone back to Hack and turned to Ghost. "That was Charlie. The woman who was scheduled to go with the field trip got sick and couldn't make it. Charlie offered to go with them."

Ghost stiffened. "When are they leaving?"

Garner looked at him. "Now. Do you want to try to catch up to them?"

Ghost hesitated. He didn't have transportation to follow the bus and if he risked running to the community center, he might miss them. Apparently Charlie wanted a little more time to herself without him. "No."

"She should be all right. No one was expecting her to be on that field trip."

"I guess it will have to be all right."

"You could take my SUV if you want to follow and make sure they're safe," Garner offered.

"No." Ghost shook his head. Charlie hadn't wanted him along. "Let's go see what's in that mine."

Garner grabbed his keys. "We can go in my vehicle." He stopped at a large safe near the door and twisted the combination back and forth until it clicked and he opened it. Inside was an arsenal of weapons. He reached in and pulled out an AR-15 military-grade rifle and handed it to Ghost. "We don't know what we're in for at the mine. If they have stashed something illegal or deadly, they might have guards positioned there." He reached in again and handed Caveman another AR-15. To Hawkeye, he handed a specially equipped sniper rifle with a high-powered scope.

Then he moved to a footlocker beside the safe and unlocked the padlock with a key and threw it open. Inside were rifle magazines and boxes of ammunition.

"Most of the magazines are already loaded. Grab what you think you might need. You can load everything into these duffel bags. We don't want to alarm the natives as we carry them out to the SUV."

Ghost wasn't sure what they'd run into at the mine. Being armed to the teeth was better than being outgunned.

Once they had everything they could possibly need for a prolonged standoff with a small army, they headed out the door and down the steps.

Caveman carried the duffel bag with the rifles, Ghost and Garner carried gym bags filled with ammo. Hawkeye carried the case with the sniper rifle. One by one, they loaded them into the back of Garner's SUV.

With the smell of weapons oil in his nostrils and the hard shell of armored plating strapped around his chest beneath his shirt, Ghost closed the hatch.

He'd started around the side of the SUV when an explosion rocked the street.

Ghost automatically dropped to the ground and rolled beneath the SUV. His pulse pounded and flashbacks threatened to overwhelm him with memories he preferred to forget.

For a moment, he was back in that Afghan village, being fired on by a Soviet-made rocket-propelled grenade launcher manned by a Taliban fighter positioned on top of one of the stick-and-mud buildings. He lay pressed to the ground, trying to breathe past the panic paralyzing his lungs.

Chapter Thirteen

Charlie sat beside Brenda Larson in the front seat of the bus headed north toward Yellowstone National Park, wondering what Kevin had found that they'd needed to see. Though she knew Ghost had their best interests at heart, she would have liked to have been there to gauge for herself the importance of the new information.

They were ten miles out of town and the children had settled back in their seats when Brenda hit her with, "So what's up between you and Jon Caspar?"

"What do you mean?" Charlie stalled, not really wanting to talk about Ghost or what was or wasn't happening between them.

"He's back. You're in love." Brenda sat back, her brows raised, her gaze direct, unflinching. "When can we expect an announcement?"

"There won't be an announcement." Charlie stared out the window, her chest tight, her eyes stinging. A tear slipped free and trailed down her cheek. Damn. And she'd promised herself she wouldn't cry that day. The field trip was all about the kids, not her pathetic excuse for a love life. She swiped at the tear and grit her teeth to keep others from falling, hoping Brenda wouldn't see them. Then she glanced at her reflection in the window and Brenda's beside it. Too late, Brenda could see everything in her reflection.

Her friend laid a hand on her arm. "What's wrong, Charlie?"

What was the use holding back now? And she really needed a shoulder to lean on. "He's going to leave again and I love him."

Brenda's face brightened. "Maybe he'll take you with him? Not that I want you to leave Grizzly Pass. Friends our age are hard to come by around here."

"He doesn't think his life is conducive to having a family." Charlie sniffed and wished her voice hadn't sounded so wobbly.

Brenda tilted her head to the side and touched her finger to her chin. "He might have a point. They move around a lot."

Charlie frowned. "You're not helping. Besides, I already knew that."

"He's a Navy SEAL. They are in a high-risk job. He might get killed on a deployment." Brenda smiled. "Perhaps he doesn't want you to be just another military widow."

"He won't give me that choice."

"Would you be okay with him staying in the military?"

"Of course."

"Would you move to be with him when he's not deployed?"

Charlie nodded.

Brenda raised her hands, palms up. "Then what's the problem?"

"He hasn't asked." Another tear slipped down her cheek.

"Have you given him a chance?" Brenda chuckled. "I've seen you when you get all stubborn and hardheaded. It's pretty intimidating."

Charlie thought about how she'd shut Ghost down the night before and how she hadn't encouraged a frank conversation since. "Maybe not."

"Then wipe your tears, have fun with the kids today and when you get home, hit him up with how you feel. If he feels the same, he'll ask you to go with him. If he doesn't, at least you will know and you can stop crying over him."

"You're right." Charlie wiped her tears and straightened, forcing a smile to her face.

She squeezed her friend's hand. "Thank you. I needed someone to talk to."

"Glad to help. Anytime."

The bus lurched, flinging her forward.

Kids screamed and the brakes smoked.

"What the—" Charlie glanced up in time to see a big, army-style dump truck straddling the highway in the middle of a curve.

The bus driver had jammed his foot on the brake and now stood on it in an attempt to stop the bus before it slammed into the truck.

"Hold on!" Charlie yelled and braced for impact.

Brakes smoked and the bus skidded across the pavement toward the truck. With a bluff on one side and a drop-off on the other, they didn't have a choice.

As if in slow motion, the bus went from fast to slow, the truck rising up before them, filling the windshield. Charlie braced herself, but couldn't close her eyes as the bus slowed, slowed, slowed but not fast enough for her. Just when she thought they would crash into the truck, the bus stopped, its front bumper scraping the side of the truck.

When the smoke from the brakes cleared, Charlie sat up and glanced back at the children, her gaze darting to the seat Lolly had occupied with Ashley Cramer and Chelsea Smith. At first she didn't see them. Then, one by one, their heads popped up over the top of the back of the seat in front of them and they looked around.

The rest of the children crawled up off the floor and into their seats, some crying, others looking frightened and disoriented.

Brenda stood and walked toward the back. "Hey, guys. Everyone okay?"

Most children nodded. One little boy shook his head, his nose bleeding, tears streaming down his cheeks.

"Come here, Elijah." Brenda gathered him up into her arms. "For now, stay in your seats until we figure out what's going on. Everything will be all right."

Charlie leaned over the back of the seat and touched the bus driver, Mr. Green's, shoulder. "Are you all right?"

He nodded. "Didn't see that coming." The old man wiped the sweat from his brow and peered through the windshield. "That could have been really bad."

Charlie looked to either side of the truck for a driver to find out why the truck was parked in the middle of a dangerous curve. Movement around the rear of the truck captured her attention and she watched as a man emerged, wearing camouflage pants, camouflage jacket and a black ski mask. He carried a military-grade rifle with a black grip and stock and he was headed straight for the door of the bus.

Charlie's heart fluttered and a cold chill shivered down her spine. "This doesn't look good. I think the truck is the least of our worries."

Another man dressed from head to toe in camouflage followed the first, also wearing a ski mask and carrying a rifle with a curved magazine loaded in it.

They stopped at the bus door.

"Open the door," the guy in front ordered.

The bus driver shook his head, shoved the shift in Reverse and pressed the accelerator.

"Go. Go. Go!" Charlie said.

He popped the clutch in his hurry and the bus engine stalled.

The men holding the rifles pointed them at the door and opened fire.

Charlie staggered backward, the seat hit her in the backs of her knees and she sat hard.

Mr. Green grunted and slumped forward over the steering wheel.

One of the men kicked what was left of the door open and entered the bus. "Stay down and don't move!" he yelled and waved his rifle at the occupants of the bus.

Charlie wanted to go to Mr. Green, but was afraid if she moved, the attackers would open fire in her direction and hit one of the children. So she stayed down, praying Lolly would remain seated.

The second man entered the bus, pulled the driver out of his seat and dragged him to the side. Then he slipped into the driver's seat and started the engine.

The dump truck engine roared to life. The big vehicle turned away from them and lumbered north along the highway until they reached a dirt road on the left. The truck turned onto the road and disappeared between the trees.

Charlie held her breath, as the bus turned as well and followed the dirt road the truck had taken. She wanted to go to Lolly and hold her in her arms, but she didn't want to draw any attention to herself or the children.

The kids sat in silence or softly sobbing, holding on to the seatbacks in front of them as they bounced along the rutted road.

Where were they going? What was going to happen to the children?

Charlie wished Ghost was with them. He'd know what to do. With only two men wielding guns, surely he would have been able to subdue them before they shot Mr. Green. She glanced down at the old bus driver, her stomach knotting.

The man's face was even paler than before and his chest didn't appear to be moving. Dear God, he was dead.

Charlie closed her eyes briefly and prayed for a miracle. Then she opened them and focused on the road ahead. She had to keep her wits about her to ensure the safety of the children.

The bus slowed around a curve in the dirt road and came to an open clearing, facing a giant hill that had been carved away at the base. It appeared to be an old mine.

The hills and mountains of Wyoming were dotted with the remnants of old gold mines from the gold rush era of the 1860s. This was just one of many that had been abandoned when the gold played out.

The man driving the bus slowed, as he headed toward the entrance to the mine.

Charlie leaned forward, her heart leaping into her throat. "What are you doing?"

"Shut up!" the man wielding the rifle backhanded her, knocking her across the seat.

She picked herself up and watched in horror as he drove right up to the mine, parking the bus so that the door opened into the mine entrance.

The driver parked the bus and clicked on a flashlight.

"Everyone out!" he yelled. He grabbed Mr. Green and dragged him down the steps and into the mine.

Charlie pressed a hand to her bruised cheek. "What are you going to do with us?"

"You have two choices—shut up and get out, or die." He pointed his rifle at her chest.

She raised her hands. "I'm getting out." Charlie eased to the edge of her seat. The rifleman backed up, giving her enough room to pass.

For a moment, she thought of all the self-defense classes she'd taken. None of them had prepared her for the possibility of children being used as target practice or shields. Her instinct was to jam her elbow into the man's gut and shove the heel of her palm into his nose. But she couldn't. If he jerked his finger on the trigger, he could shoot a kid.

Charlie could never live with herself if her actions were the cause of one of these babies being killed. She glanced back at Lolly as she stepped down off the bus.

The man with the flashlight waved Charlie to the side. "Do something stupid and one of these kids will get hurt."

She raised her hands. "Please don't hurt the children. Just tell me what you want me to do. I'll do it."

"Stand over there and keep quiet." He shone the flashlight toward a stack of crates.

Charlie followed the beam and stopped when the light swung back toward the bus.

Three children dropped down from the bus, huddling together, sniffling in the dark. The flashlight swung her way.

Charlie opened her arms and the kids ran into them.

She counted them as they emerged, one by one. When Lolly reached the ground, she looked for her mother.

Charlie nearly cried. Again the flashlight swung her way and Lolly ran to her. Charlie held her in her arms, smoothing her hand over her hair. "It's going to be all right," she whispered. "I promise." Somehow they'd get out of this in one piece. She refused to break her promise to her daughter.

Brenda brought up the rear with Lolly's friends Chelsea and Ashley.

Another man joined the two in camouflage. This one was dressed all in black with a matching black ski mask. He stood beside the other two as Brenda walked by with the two little girls.

He grabbed Ashley and swung her up into his arms. "I'll take this one."

Brenda leaped forward. "Don't you hurt her!"

The man with the flashlight swung it, clipping Brenda in the side of the head.

Brenda crumpled to the ground and lay still.

Chelsea dropped down beside her, crying hysterically.

"Take the brat before I hit her, too," Flashlight Guy shouted.

Charlie rushed forward and dragged Chelsea back to where the rest of the children huddled. She told them to stay where they were and then she eased forward to where Brenda lay with her face down, her eyes closed.

"Get back!" the man with the gun yelled.

Charlie inched back to stand with the cluster of

kids and waited for the men to leave or at least back up enough to let her get to Brenda and the bus driver.

The bus moved away from the opening of the mine and a triangle of sunlight shone in.

Charlie studied everything around her, looking for an escape route, counting the number of men involved, evaluating her options and coming up with no plan that would save twenty children.

Yet another man wearing camouflage stepped into the cave entrance where the original captors stood. He was bigger than first two, and he carried a 9 millimeter pistol. "Where's Cramer?"

"Hell if I know. He drove the truck," Flashlight man said.

"He was here a minute ago," the rifleman said. "Took one of the kids and walked out."

The man muttered a curse. "Dalton, find him. Vern, help me move the plate in place."

"What about them?" Vern said.

"If one of them moves, we'll shoot them," the big man said.

Based on the names they were calling each other, Charlie knew who they were. The Vanders brothers. And it appeared Tim Cramer had come along for the ride in order to steal his daughter away. Charlie would bet Cramer had already escaped the compound with his girl. Dalton wouldn't find them.

For the next few minutes, the two men worked to

move a huge metal plate into position over the entrance of the mine.

Charlie took the opportunity to study the boxes lining the walls. She reached into an open one. Inside were sticks of dynamite and dozens of empty cartridge boxes. She searched for a weapon among the boxes, only to find more empty boxes. Another crate contained empty cases of what appeared to have at one time contained new AR-15s. More than the number carried by the men holding them hostage. A lot more. In one crate alone, she counted over twenty empty AR-15 boxes. And there were a lot of crates lining the walls of the mine. What were they planning? A total takeover of the state?

Once the metal door was in place, most of the light was blocked. A little at the top and sides gave just enough for Charlie to make it over to Brenda and Mr. Green. She felt for a pulse on the bus driver. His skin was cold, he lay very still and no matter how long Charlie pressed her fingers to the base of his throat, she couldn't find a pulse. The man was dead.

Her heart hurt for his wife. They were a childless couple who loved each other and their menagerie of dogs.

Moving to Brenda she touched the caregiver's shoulder. "Brenda."

Brenda moaned.

"Sweetie, please. Wake up and tell me you're all right."

She moaned again and rolled onto her back. "Why is it so dark?" she croaked.

"We're in a mine."

"Oh, God." She tried to lift her head but dropped it back to the ground. "The kids?"

"All here and okay, except Ashley Cramer."

"Where's she?" She rolled to her side and tried to push to a sitting position. "Linnea will be frantic."

"I think Tim took her."

"That bastard." Brenda pressed her hand to her lips. "Sorry."

Charlie wanted to say a whole string of curses, but it wouldn't get them out of the mess they were in. "Tim was in on this."

"What is *this*, anyway?" Brenda asked, blinking her eyes before staring around at the walls of the mine.

"The Vanders brothers have taken us hostage. We're in some mine shaft."

"Those idiots?" She tried to get up, but couldn't quite make it on her own. "What do they hope to accomplish?"

"I don't know." Charlie helped Brenda to her feet and she staggered over to the children where she collapsed to a sitting position.

The children gathered around her, all wanting to

be held and comforted, every one of them frightened out of their minds.

Charlie knelt beside Lolly. "Are you doing okay?"

She nodded. "Are those bad men going to let us out of this cave?"

"I don't know if they will, but someone will find us and let us out." She hoped it was true. As far as she knew, nobody would know where to look for them.

"Mr. Caspar will find us. He's a real hero."

Charlie hugged her close. "Yes, Lolly, he is." That's what he did. He fought for his country. For her and Lolly and everyone else. He was the real hero.

"Miss Brenda told me." Lolly snuggled against Charlie. "I'm cold."

Charlie rubbed her arms and pulled her closer.

"I hope my daddy comes soon."

Charlie swallowed the lump in her throat to say, "Your daddy?" Had she overheard them talking about her? Had she put the pieces together and guessed?

"Mr. Caspar. He's nice and he's a hero. I want him to be my daddy."

"Oh, baby." Charlie held her tight and fought the tears. She wanted Ghost to be Lolly's daddy, too. And Charlie wanted him to be her husband. If she had another chance, she'd get right to the point and ask him if he would marry them. If he said no, she'd figure out how to live without him. But on the slim chance he said yes, she'd be the happiest woman alive and follow him to the ends of the earth, if that's what it took.

"WHAT THE HELL was that?" Caveman called out from behind a parked pickup.

The sound of the Delta Force soldier's voice penetrated the fog of memories and yanked Ghost back to the present and Grizzly Pass, Wyoming.

Caveman and Hawkeye had sought cover behind vehicles while Garner knelt near the corner of a brick building. Ghost waited a moment, trying to determine where the sound had come from. When no other explosions shook the ground, he rolled from beneath the SUV and stood.

"Sounded like it came from the south end of town," Garner said.

A siren wailed from the north, heading toward the tavern.

Ghost hurried toward the front of the building in time to see a sheriff's vehicle racing south along Main Street.

"Come on," Garner said. "Let's go check it out."

All four men climbed into the SUV and took off after the sheriff.

At the other end of town people were coming out of their homes and businesses, standing in clumps, talking to each other, holding their small children close. The sheriff's car was positioned at the end of Main Street, blocking traffic from entering or leaving town.

Garner parked a block away. The men piled out and hurried toward one of the abandoned buildings on the edge of town. The front wall had been blown out, the bricks scattered across the street.

Behind them, another siren sounded and the volunteer fire department engine truck rolled down the street, passing them to stop next to the sheriff's vehicle. Firefighters jumped to the ground and started unrolling a long hose.

The sheriff emerged from the building, covered in dust, shaking his head. "You won't need that. Looks like someone set off a stick of dynamite. No fire, no smoke, just a big mess."

Ghost inhaled and let out a long, slow breath and asked, "Why?" He turned to Garner and the others. "Why would someone want to blow up an old building in a little town?"

"Kids bored in the middle of summer?" Caveman offered.

No. Ghost wasn't buying it. Someone had deliberately set that dynamite to blow in that particular building at that particular time.

"It didn't do much damage." Hawkeye studied the scene. "It was an old building not worth anything.

Whoever did it, did the town a favor, getting the demolition started."

"Why would they pick this building on the south end of town?" Ghost asked, his mind wrapping around the possibilities and coming up with one. "Unless they were creating a diversion to draw all of the attention away from something."

The radio clipped to Sheriff Scott's shoulder chirped with static. "Sheriff, we have a problem," came the tinny voice.

Sheriff Scott touched the mic. "Give it to me."

Ghost's attention zeroed in on that radio and what was being said, his gut clenching.

"Someone's demanding LeRoy Vanders's release."

"Demanding?" The sheriff snorted. "On what grounds?"

"They want to negotiate his release in exchange for a busload of our kids."

The words hit Ghost like a punch in the gut.

The sheriff's face paled and everyone standing in hearing range of the sheriff's radio froze.

"What is he asking for?" Sheriff Scott asked.

"He wants you to bring LeRoy Vanders to Lucky Lou's Gold Mine in one hour, in a helicopter. If you aren't there in exactly one hour, they will blow up the entrance to the old mine with dynamite. With the children inside."

Ghost grabbed Garner's arm. "That's my woman and my kid on that bus."

"We have to work with the sheriff to get those kids to safety," Garner said. He stepped toward Sheriff Scott. "Sir."

"Don't bother me now. I have a crisis to avert." The sheriff hit his mic. "Who the hell can we call with a helicopter?"

Garner got in front of the sheriff. "I can get one in under an hour."

The sheriff looked at Garner and nodded. Then he keyed the mic. "Get Vanders ready. I'll let you know when the helicopter lands." He stared at Garner. "If you're wrong, you might cost us the lives of those kids."

"I can get one from Bozeman in thirty minutes." He gave the sheriff instructions on how to contact his resource at the Bozeman airport. A helicopter would be dispatched in less than ten minutes.

Ghost paced the pavement, desperate to do something. "We can't wait for them to make the trade. What if they decide to bury those kids in the mine anyway? They could have that whole place rigged with explosives."

"We'll make the exchange," the sheriff said. "We can't risk the lives of the children."

"Sheriff." Ghost planted himself in front of the sheriff. "You have four of the most highly skilled military men at your disposal. Let us get in there, recon the situation and report what we see."

"I don't know." The sheriff shook his head. "If they see you, they might detonate the explosives."

"We know how to get in without being seen. We can get a count on the number of combatants. You'd be better off knowing numbers in case they start shooting at the men delivering Vanders."

"He has a point," Garner added. "Let us be your eyes and ears while you're putting the exchange in place."

The sheriff stared at Garner. "How do I know you won't do something stupid?"

Ghost grabbed the man's arm. "The woman I love and my little girl were on that bus. I wouldn't do anything that would cause them harm. Please. Let us do this."

The sheriff stared into Ghost's face. "I've known you for a long time. I knew your father. He was proud that you made it through SEAL training. From what they say, only the best of the best can be a SEAL." He stared at the others. "I trust Jon Caspar. If he trusts you, I guess I have to, as well. Go."

Ghost turned to run.

The sheriff snagged his arm. "We have to bring those kids back alive. One of them is my grandson."

Ghost nodded and took off for the DHS agent's SUV. Hawkeye, Garner and Cavemen beat him to it, climbing in. Ghost settled in the seat and leaned forward, staring through the front windshield as they blew through town and north toward Lucky Lou's Gold Mine. He prayed they could get in without being seen and that none of the passengers on the bus had been hurt in the hostage takeover.

Chapter Fourteen

Lolly fell asleep, leaning against Charlie.

Unable to sit still without coming up with a plan, she eased Lolly to the floor and stood, stretching the kinks out of her muscles. She wondered how long it had been since they'd been captured. Thirty minutes? An hour? More?

Some children were still sniffling, huddled up to Brenda, seeking comfort from each other.

Charlie crossed to the metal plate covering the opening of the mine and strained to hear what was happening outside.

"They'll be here on time if they want to see those kids again," a voice said.

Charlie recognized it as the man who'd been carrying the flashlight, Dalton Vanders.

"What if they bring in the feds?" The slower, deeper voice of Vernon Vanders said. "We aren't equipped for a standoff."

"We have the detonators." The third voice could only be the man in charge. The oldest of the Vanders brothers, GW. "The mine entrance is rigged to blow. If they don't give us what we want, we blow the entrance."

Charlie gasped. If they blew the entrance, everyone inside could be buried alive. Should, by some miracle, they live through the blast, they might suffocate before anyone could dig them out.

"They better hope they bring Dad in that helicopter," Dalton said.

"Ten minutes. If they don't show by then, we blow and go," GW said, his voice moving away from the mine entrance.

Ten minutes. Charlie looked around in the limited lighting. They had ten minutes to figure out how to get out of the mine.

Going deeper without lights was suicide. They could fall down open vertical shafts in the floor, or die due to poisonous gases. She went back to the boxes and searched for something, anything she could use to move the door enough they could slip out.

The only thing she could find was a broken slat from one of the crates. If she could use it as leverage, she might be able to move the heavy metal plate that had taken two men to slide in place.

Charlie jammed the slat into the sunlit gap at the

base of the metal barrier. Holding on to the end, she leaned back as hard as she could, putting all of her weight into it. The plate budged, but only half an inch. She pulled the slat out and lay down on the floor.

She could see a little bit of daylight and movement. A couple of yards from the entrance, stood someone wearing camouflage pants and black work boots.

She didn't know where the others were, but she couldn't wait for them to appear. She had to get a wide enough gap to slip the children out and away from the men before they got really stupid and detonated the charges that would seal twenty children and the adults in the mine.

Fitting the slat back in the gap, she pulled again, the gap widening until a four-inch opening stretched from the top to the bottom of the entrance.

On her third attempt, the slat cracked and broke. Charlie fell on her butt with a bone-jarring thud and groaned. The additional space she'd gained was less than another inch. Five inches wide might get a small child out, but not Brenda and Charlie. And the children would need to be guided into the nearby trees and underbrush to hide. Without the leverage of the slat, she'd have to work with her bare hands. As heavy as the metal plate was, she doubted she'd get far, but she had to try.

The sky darkened, as if clouds had blocked the sun.

Charlie crawled to the widened gap and peered out. She spotted all three Vanders brothers. They stood near the dump truck. Two of them held the AR-15s. The one she figured was GW had the 9 millimeter in a holster on his hip and his hand wrapped around a small gadget Charlie assumed was the detonator.

Her teeth ground together. Any man who could contemplate blowing up the entrance to a mine with children trapped inside was no man at all. He was an animal.

She looked to her right and her left. If she remembered correctly from their drive in, the mine entrance had several bushes growing next to it and a young tree sprouting near the base of the hill. If they could get the kids to the bushes they might make it to the forest before their escape was discovered. The men outside must have felt pretty confident in the ability of the rusty metal plate holding their hostages inside. Either that or they were too busy watching for whatever they'd demanded to arrive to keep a close eye on a bunch of kids and two women.

Charlie leaped to her feet. Time was running out. She had to get the children to safety before the crazy brothers sealed their fates inside a mine shaft tomb.

Brenda disentangled herself from the children and rose to assist. "Let me help," she said.

With her heart pumping adrenaline through her veins, Charlie grabbed the metal plate.

Brenda curled her fingers around the rusty steel.

Together they leaned back, straining to move the heavy sheet of metal. By God, they'd move that barrier if it was the last thing they did.

Charlie prayed it wasn't.

ARMED WITH A headset radio and an AR-15 rifle, Ghost lived up to his nickname and eased up to the edge of the mine compound, clinging to the brush. "Three targets, two carrying rifles and one with the prize."

"I got one vehicle leaving by road." Caveman was working his way toward the mine by paralleling the road in and out. "Notifying 911. They have the state highway patrol on standby. They should pick him up on the highway."

"I'm in position in the bird's nest," Hawkeye said from his position on a ridge high above the mine clearing.

"Ready when you are," Garner added.

The big guy in the middle had his fist closed around a small box of some sort. If it was a detonator, they'd have to get him to let go of it before they took out the other two men. It would do no good to kill any of them, if the guy holding the key to the show pressed that button.

He studied the layout. An older model dump truck was parked a couple of yards away from the mine entrance. One of the men stood near the rear of the truck, watching the road in. Another used the other end of the truck as cover, also monitoring the only road in.

The man with his hand on the detonator pulled what appeared to be a satellite phone off the web harness he wore and hit several buttons.

"Where's Vanders and our bird?" he demanded. "My thumb is a hair's breadth away from the ignition button." He listened for a moment. "I don't care if it takes time to get a helicopter here. Five minutes. That's all that's left between you and those kids. Five." He jabbed the phone, ending the call. "Get ready. Either they'll show up with him and the bird, or we set off some fireworks and get the hell out of here."

"I think I hear something coming," one of the men shouted.

"'Bout time," the guy at the other end of the truck said. "I need a beer."

The sound of rotor blades beating the air came over the top of the hill.

"Got my sights on the prize holder," Hawkeye reported.

"Do not engage," Garner reiterated the sheriff's instructions. He was positioned to the right of Ghost and twenty yards to his rear. He was to transfer data to the sheriff as the others took their positions.

"Holding steady," Hawkeye reassured.

Ghost scanned the area for other bad guys but was surprised there were only three. It didn't take an army to take a school bus full of children and unarmed adults. And with the lives of those children held in the balance, these men could demand the world and get it.

The helicopter crested the hill and hovered over the mine.

"What are they waiting for?" one of the men shouted.

"I don't know," the man holding the detonator yelled back over the roar of the helicopter.

"There's someone with a gun in there!" One of the men with a rifle pointed his weapon at the helicopter.

"Don't shoot!" detonator man yelled.

"They've got a gun!" He raised his weapon to his shoulder and fired.

Ghost shook his head. Just what they needed, a trigger-happy bad guy firing at the helicopter carrying their bargaining chip. "The situation has escalated, request permission to move in and take out the targets," Ghost said.

"Sheriff said do not engage," Garner reminded him.

"The sheriff didn't get the word to the bad guys.

Things are about to get really bad." Ghost bunched his muscles, ready to charge into the gray.

"I've got the shooter in my sights," Hawkeye reminded them.

"I'm in position and have the other dude with the gun in mine," Caveman said.

Ghost couldn't wait for the men to freak out and blow up the mine entrance. "I'm going in for the man with the prize. Boss, either you're with me or you're not."

"I got your six, coming up on your left," Garner said. "Sheriff gave the go-ahead. They're lifting off."

As the helicopter climbed higher into the sky, the team moved in.

Hawkeye took out the man firing at the bird. Caveman fired at the other, nicked his leg and sent him to the ground. Unfortunately, he still had his gun in hand and was firing back in the direction of Caveman.

Ghost was almost across the open ground when the man with the detonator turned toward the mine entrance and raised his hand.

Making a flying tackle, Ghost hit the man in his midsection, sending him staggering backward. He stumbled and hit the ground flat on his back. The detonator flew from his grasp and skittered across the dry ground, landing in front of the man firing at Caveman.

He flung his rifle to the ground and low-crawled toward the detonator.

Ghost punched the man he'd tackled in the nose and scrambled to his feet, flinging himself at the man as he reached for the detonator.

Before he could get to him, the man's hand slammed down on the red button.

The world erupted behind Ghost, sending him flying forward and slamming him to the ground. He laid for a moment, stunned, his ears ringing. The man who'd hit the button lifted his head and stared at him, then reached for his rifle.

Ghost lurched to his feet and kicked the rifle out of the other man's grip.

A shot rang out behind him and the big guy he'd tackled stood facing him, his eyes wide, blood spreading across his camouflage shirt. He took one step and fell forward like a tree toppled by lumber-jacks.

Garner lay on the ground nearby, his rifle up to his shoulder. "Told you I had your six."

Ghost scanned the area. Caveman came out of the woods, the helicopter dropped lower and landed on the other side of the dump truck and people rushed toward the mine entrance.

"Charlie. Lolly." Ghost's head still rang and his leg ached, but none of that mattered. The woman he loved and his only child were trapped behind the rocks and rubble blocking the entrance to the old mine.

He ran toward the jumble of boulders and rocks. Dust swirled in a cloud making it hard to see clearly. Or were those tears clouding his vision?

"Charlie! Lolly!" Oh, dear God, how was he going to get them out of there? He lifted a boulder and tossed it to the side. He lifted another and threw it to the side, too.

"Ghost!" Hawkeye said his name several times before he heard the sound through his headset.

"They're in there," Ghost said, his heart ripped to shreds, his mind numb. "They're in there, and I can't get to them."

"Ghost, listen to me," Hawkeye said. "I have them in my sights."

"What?" Ghost straightened from the pile of rocks. "How?"

"They're in the woods to the south of the mine. I count more than a dozen kids and two adults."

From desperation to hope, Ghost left the rocks and ran toward the south side of the mine. He crashed through brush, tripped over logs and fell several times before he spotted something pink through the dense foliage.

When he broke through the underbrush, he stumbled and fell to his knees in front of all the children and two women. "Charlie! Lolly!" He coughed, choking with the dust he'd inhaled and the emotion he couldn't hold back.

"Ghost?" Charlie ran forward and knelt beside him. "Is that you?" She rubbed her hands across his face, her fingers getting coated with a fine layer of dust. "Oh, thank God." She flung her arms around him and kissed him, dirt and all.

He held her close for a long time. His leg hurt like hell and his ears still rang, but Charlie, Lolly and the rest of the kids were okay.

"Mr. Caspar?" Lolly inched forward, her brows knit, her cheeks streaked with dried tears.

"Lolly, baby, come here." He held out an arm, making room for her in his embrace.

She ran to him and wrapped her arms around his neck. "I was so scared."

He laughed. "So was I." He kissed her cheek with a loud smack. "But we're okay now."

She leaned back and stared at his face. "You're dirty."

He laughed out loud, his heart filled with so much joy, he was afraid it might explode. "Yes, I am. And I'm so happy you and your mama are all right."

Her eyes filled with tears. "Mr. Green didn't come out with us."

Charlie smoothed a hand over her hair. "No, sweetie, he didn't. But the sheriff will make sure they get him out of there. You'll see."

Ghost's gaze connected with Charlie's.

"The bus driver," she whispered and shook her head, her eyes filling.

He nodded. With Charlie's help, Ghost lurched to his feet and straightened his leg, the pain shooting up into his hip. He ignored it, looking at the children huddled around another young woman. He shook his head, thankful they were all alive. "How did you get them out of the mine?"

Charlie held up her hands, stained with rust and marked with cuts and scrapes. "Brenda and I moved the metal plate they'd used to block the entrance. They thought it could keep a couple of women with a bunch of children contained." She snorted. "They didn't count on the adrenaline rush we'd get at the mention of blowing the entrance." Charlie lifted her chin and smiled at the other woman. "The important thing is, we got it open enough to get all of the children out while the Vanders brothers were shooting at the helicopter. It was close, but we were able to get all of the children out of the mine before the explosion."

Ghost shook his head, a grin spreading across his face. "You are amazing."

"And you should have seen Lolly, herding the kids into single file like the little soldier she is." Charlie smiled down at their daughter. "She's so much like you it hurts sometimes."

Lolly stared up at Ghost. "Mr. Caspar, will you be my daddy?"

Her words hit Ghost in the gut and he sucked in a breath before responding. "I don't know." He turned to Charlie. "What does your mother think about the idea?"

Charlie's eyes filled again, tears spilled over the edges and her bottom lip trembled. "I was going to wait until I was wearing a pretty dress and my hair was fixed." She stared down at her wrecked hands. "And after a manicure." She laughed, the sound coming out as more of a sob. "But I don't want to wait another minute to know." She dropped to one knee and took Ghost's hand.

"What are you doing?" he asked. He tried to lift her back to her feet, but she resisted.

"Jon Caspar, you big, sexy SEAL, with a heart as big as the Wyoming sky, will you make an honest woman of me and marry me?" She stared up at him, tears running down her dirty face, her hair a riot of uncontrollable curls, her clothes torn and smeared with rust. She was the most beautiful woman in the world.

Ghost's heart swelled in his chest to the point he thought it could no longer be contained.

Lolly clapped her hands together, her eyes alight with excitement. "Please say yes!"

Ghost laughed and drew Charlie up into his

arms. "I would have liked a shower before I pro-posed to you. But since we're here, the sun is shin-ing and I'm holding the most beautiful woman in the world, I can't think of a better answer than yes." He drew in a deep breath and bent to kiss the tip of her nose. "Yes, I'll marry you. Yes, I'd love to have Lolly as my very own daughter. And yes, we'll work things out, somehow, because that's what people do who love each other as much as we do. I love you, Charlie, from the tips of my toes to my very last breath."

"Jon, I've always loved you," Charlie said. "From our first date, I knew you were the one for me. I just had to wait until *you* knew I was the one for you."

He brushed a strand of her hair out of her face and tucked it behind her ear. "I've always loved you, but I didn't want to hurt you by dragging you through the life of a SEAL's wife."

Charlie laughed. "So you hurt me by leaving me behind?" She shook her head. "That's man think-ing." She cupped his face and leaned up on her toes to kiss him. "I'd follow you to the ends of the earth, and I'd always be there for you when you came back from deployment."

"Me, too." Lolly hugged him around his knees. "I love you, too. I'm going to have a daddy of my own." She looked up at him with his blue eyes and her mother's red hair and grinned. "We're going to be a family."

"You bet, we are." Ghost lifted her up on his arm and wrapped the other around Charlie. Together, they led the others out of the woods and back to the clearing in front of the mine.

CHARLIE FELT AS if she'd gone from one movie set to the other and wondered if she had been dreaming through all that had happened. She had a hard time wrapping her mind around all of it from having the bus hijacked to being trapped in a mine, to the fairy-tale proposal in the woods and back to the cacophony of every kind of motor vehicle and dozens of uniformed personnel filling her vision.

A fire truck had arrived, along with rescue vehicles from across the county. Every sheriff's deputy on duty was there along with the Wyoming Highway Patrol. The sheriff was in the middle of all of it speaking with the DHS representative, Kevin Garner.

When Charlie emerged from the woods with Ghost, Brenda and all of the children, a round of applause erupted from the rescue personnel.

Paramedics rushed forward to check out the children, Brenda and Charlie.

She suffered through the delay of having her hands cleaned and bandaged, while Ghost carried

Lolly over to where the sheriff directed the remaining efforts.

Charlie hurried over as soon as she could break away.

Tim Cramer was tucked into the backseat of one of the Wyoming Highway Patrol cars, his face angry, his hands cuffed behind him.

A deputy escorted a pale and shaky Linnea Cramer into the fray where she was reunited with her daughter, Ashley, in a tearful reunion.

"Thank God, they got Ashley back," Charlie said as she joined the group gathered around the sheriff.

"We had a roadblock set up on the highway headed toward Montana. We figured he'd make a run for Canada with the child," the sheriff said. "Wyoming Highway Patrol picked him up. If he thought he had problems before, he's in a heap more trouble now. Rebecca Florence came to this morning and said it was Tim Cramer who'd attacked her in the library. He'd worn the ski mask he was found with today, but she knew it was him when he told her it was her fault he was losing his wife."

Charlie frowned. "What do you mean it was her fault? I didn't think she and Linnea were even friends."

The sheriff's mouth twisted. "Apparently, Ms. Florence was in Bozeman for a library conference staying at the same hotel where Cramer was entertaining a young lady who wasn't his wife in a room on the same floor as Rebecca's."

"And she told Linnea." Charlie nodded. "So he beat her up for squealing on him."

The sheriff nodded.

"What about the Vanders brothers?" Charlie asked, looking around as paramedics loaded a sheet-draped body into the back of one of the waiting ambulances.

"Dalton is dead, Vernon and GW will live to face time in the state prison," the sheriff said.

Charlie couldn't feel sorry for any of them. How long would it be before the children got over the terror they'd faced on the bus and in the dark mine? "I hope they get what they deserve."

Ghost slipped an arm around her.

She leaned into his strength, glad he was there.

"If not for Garner's team, it could have been a whole lot worse," Sheriff Scott said. "The chopper took hits from Dalton's gun. The pilot is being treated for a gunshot wound to his leg and Dalton shot his own father." The sheriff shook his head. "LeRoy Vanders took a bullet to the chest. They're working on him now and loading him into the helicopter his son tried to shoot down. I doubt he'll make it all the way to the hospital in Bozeman."

"What about Mr. Green?" Charlie asked. Her heart ached for the old man who'd done nothing to deserve being killed for driving a busload of kids.

"He's still inside the mine." She shook her head. "He didn't make it. Vernon took him out on the bus."

The sheriff's lips thinned and released a long sigh. "His wife will be devastated." He pinched the bridge of his nose before continuing. "I ordered excavation equipment in case we had to dig you and the kids out. It's on its way. We'll get him out."

Charlie nodded.

Sheriff Scott shot a glance at the crumbled mine entrance. "What I don't understand is where they got all the explosives and detonators."

Ghost's jaw tightened. "From what I saw of the detonator, it was military grade. I knew the Vanderses had an arsenal of guns from all the hunting they do. But the explosives are an entirely different game."

Charlie touched the sheriff's arm. "I found at least a dozen wooden crates in the mine. They were filled with empty boxes from what appeared to be a large number of rifles, boxes of ammo and the curved magazines I've seen used with the semiautomatic weapons the military use. What would the Vanders brothers need with that many weapons?"

"Unless they aren't the only ones stockpiling weapons," Kevin Garner said. "We have infrared satellite photos of a group of people unloading items from a truck into the mine. It was from only a few days ago."

"Those crates were empty except for the boxes the weapons came in."

"Where did all of those guns and ammo go?" the sheriff asked. "And who shipped all of them? There has to be a paper or money trail."

Garner nodded. "I have my tech guy working on that. In the meantime, getting into that mine and going through those crates might help us trace the weapons back to the buyer."

The sheriff's face grew grim. "Sounds like someone is trying to build an army."

"Then we better find out who before they succeed," Garner said.

Charlie shivered in the warm country air. Her peaceful hometown of Grizzly Pass, Wyoming, had darker secrets than she'd ever expected. She began to wonder if bringing her daughter there to raise had been a good idea after all.

Ghost tightened his hold around her waist, reminding her that if she hadn't come back, she wouldn't have found Ghost again.

Everything happened for a reason. And she couldn't be happier that she now had her family back together. Whatever the future held, wherever they went, it would be as a family. Anything else, they could deal with, as long as they were together.

An hour later, Kevin Garner loaded his team

of specialists into his SUV along with Charlie and Lolly and took them back to town.

He dropped Charlie, Lolly and Ghost at the community center where Charlie had left her Jeep.

Charlie handed over her keys. "If you don't mind, my hands are shaking too much to drive."

He took the keys in exchange for a kiss and helped her and Lolly into the vehicle.

Once they were all inside, he glanced over at Charlie and took her hand. "Just so you know, I plan on staying until the situation is resolved here in Grizzly Pass. After that, I hope you'll be patient and flexible with where we go next."

Charlie squeezed his fingers. "I'm one hundred percent okay with that plan. As long as you're here with us. I don't think we've found the people at the crux of what's been going on around here."

"Me either," he said. "But I know one thing."

"What's that?"

"I'm not leaving until we do. And when I do leave, you and Lolly are coming with me." He lifted her hand and pressed a kiss to the backs of her knuckles.

"Good," Charlie said. "Because I'm not letting go this time."

"How do you feel about being a Navy wife?"

"I couldn't be prouder, as long as my Navy husband is you."

"Good, because once we've completed this assignment, I want to rejoin my unit in Virginia."

"I've always wanted to go to Virginia," she said, a happy smile spreading across her face.

"And if the medical board invites me to leave the military?"

She turned her head toward him. "We could come back to Wyoming."

"I'm glad you feel that way. Being back reminded me how much I love this state. More than that, it reminded me of how much I love you."

* * * * *

MIRA®

Join FBI agent Craig Frasier and criminal psychologist Kieran Finnegan as they track down a madman who is obsessed with perfect beauty.

"Horrible! Oh, God, horrible—tragic!" John Shaw said, shaking his head with a dazed look as he sat on his bar stool at Finnegan's Pub.

Kieran nodded sympathetically. Construction crews had found old graves when they were working on the foundations at the hot new downtown venue Le Club Vampyre.

Anthropologists had found the new body among the old graves the next day.

It wasn't just *any* body.

It was the body of supermodel Jeannette Gilbert.

Finding the old graves wasn't much of a shock—not in New York City, and not in a building that was close to two centuries old. The structure that housed Le Club Vampyre was a deconsecrated Episcopal church. The church's congregation had moved to a facility it had purchased from the Catholic church—whose congregation was now in a sparkling new basilica over on Park Avenue. While many had bemoaned the fact that such a venerable old institution had been turned into an establishment for those into sex, drugs and rock and roll, life—and business—went on.

And with life going on…

Well, work on the building's foundations went on, too. It was while investigators were still being called in following the discovery of the newly deceased body—moments before it hit the news—that Kieran Finnegan learned about it, and that was because she was helping out at her family's establishment, Finnegan's on Broadway. Like the old church/nightclub behind it, Finnegan's dated back to just before the Civil War, and had been a pub for most of those years. Since it was geographically the closest place to the church with liquor, it had apparently seemed the right spot at that moment for Professor John Shaw.

A serial killer is striking a little too close to home in the second novel in the
NEW YORK CONFIDENTIAL *series,*
A PERFECT OBSESSION
coming soon from New York Times *bestselling author*
Heather Graham and MIRA Books.

REQUEST YOUR FREE BOOKS!
2 FREE NOVELS PLUS 2 FREE GIFTS!

HARLEQUIN®

INTRIGUE

BREATHTAKING ROMANTIC SUSPENSE

YES! Please send me 2 FREE Harlequin® Intrigue novels and my 2 FREE gifts (gifts are worth about $10). After receiving them, if I don't wish to receive any more books, I can return the shipping statement marked "cancel." If I don't cancel, I will receive 6 brand-new novels every month and be billed just $4.74 per book in the U.S. or $5.49 per book in Canada. That's a savings of at least 12% off the cover price! It's quite a bargain! Shipping and handling is just 50¢ per book in the U.S. and 75¢ per book in Canada.* I understand that accepting the 2 free books and gifts places me under no obligation to buy anything. I can always return a shipment and cancel at any time. Even if I never buy another book, the two free books and gifts are mine to keep forever.

182/382 HDN GH3D

Name	(PLEASE PRINT)
Address	Apt. #
City	State/Prov.	Zip/Postal Code

Signature (if under 18, a parent or guardian must sign)

Mail to the **Reader Service:**
IN U.S.A.: P.O. Box 1867, Buffalo, NY 14240-1867
IN CANADA: P.O. Box 609, Fort Erie, Ontario L2A 5X3
**Are you a subscriber to Harlequin® Intrigue books
and want to receive the larger-print edition?
Call 1-800-873-8635 or visit www.ReaderService.com.**

* Terms and prices subject to change without notice. Prices do not include applicable taxes. Sales tax applicable in N.Y. Canadian residents will be charged applicable taxes. Offer not valid in Quebec. This offer is limited to one order per household. Not valid for current subscribers to Harlequin Intrigue books. All orders subject to credit approval. Credit or debit balances in a customer's account(s) may be offset by any other outstanding balance owed by or to the customer. Please allow 4 to 6 weeks for delivery. Offer available while quantities last.

Your Privacy—The Reader Service is committed to protecting your privacy. Our Privacy Policy is available online at www.ReaderService.com or upon request from the Reader Service.

We make a portion of our mailing list available to reputable third parties that offer products we believe may interest you. If you prefer that we not exchange your name with third parties, or if you wish to clarify or modify your communication preferences, please visit us at www.ReaderService.com/consumerchoice or write to us at Reader Service Preference Service, P.O. Box 9062, Buffalo, NY 14240-9062. Include your complete name and address.

HII5

THE WORLD IS BETTER WITH

Romance

0670

Harlequin has everything from contemporary, passionate and heartwarming to suspenseful and inspirational stories.

Whatever your mood, we have a romance just for you!

Connect with us to find your next great read, special offers and more.

f /HarlequinBooks

🐦 @HarlequinBooks

www.HarlequinBlog.com

www.Harlequin.com/Newsletters

⊞ HARLEQUIN®

A *Romance* FOR EVERY MOOD™

www.Harlequin.com